1995

Something
Marvelous
Is About
to Happen

Books by James Stevenson

Something Marvelous Is About to Happen

by James Stevenson

Harper & Row, Publishers
New York, Evanston, San Francisco, London

FIRST EDITION

STANDARD BOOK NUMBER: 06-014118-2

LIBRARY OF CONGRESS CATALOG CARD
NUMBER: 71-138764

DESIGN BY VINCENT CECI

To William Shawn

The Case Against Prof. Lamberti

Early bill

"There were some real good xylophone players like the Four Avalos, Friscoes (Lou Chiha), El Celeve, the Johnsons, El Cota, the Five Musical Spillers . . . and of course to me the funniest of 'em all, the Great Lamberti, whose special bit was that while he was playing a stripteaser appeared behind him (unbeknownst to him, of course) and when the audience applauded he thought it was for him (real funny)."
— *Joe Laurie. Jr., Vaudeville: From the Honky-Tonks to the Palace*

Prof. Lamberti Onstage *(From an old photograph)*

ABOVE: The primary source for Lamberti cultists. This, plus the purported photograph, forms the basis for their belief.

Lamberti Vanishing

"[There] . . . has been . . . a general [decline] in . . . [public] [acceptance . . .] . . ."—*Anon.*

NOTE: The above sequence of pictures is regarded as one of the most telling arguments against Lamberti.*

*Pro-Lamberti forces do not accept this; in fact, they maintain that the sequence has been deliberately printed in reverse.

As far as can be determined, there has never been a Prof. Lamberti in the American Society of Professors, and, if so, no course of his was accredited; ||

—Fragment of a lengthy letter from President of American Society of Professors

Lamberti Public Acceptance Sampling

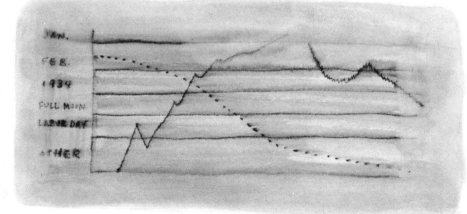

FOR   · · · · ·

AGAINST   ———

UNDECIDED   ∿∿∿∿

**Manning Makes
No Mention
of Lamberti
Whatsoever**

Engraved for Practical Book for Practical People.

James H. Manning

By James H. Manning.

THIS is preëminently the business age. N
before have commercial schemes and un
takings assumed such vast proportions. Neve
fore has the spirit of business permeated e
avenue and relation of life as it does to-day.

Business is King, and the man of affairs, is u
the moving figure on the world's stage.

He has reduced commercial interests to a sc
and has so advanced competition that high pr
is the rule, and unremitting watchfulness the p
not only of success but also of self-protection.

Every one is sooner or later swept into relat
with this modern spirit of business.

The day has gone by when man or women
without inevitable disaster, disregard the necessit
for sufficient knowledge of how to transact ordinar
business affairs.

The constantly enlarging sphere of women
modern days is making it increasingly important t
them as well as for men, to understand the for
and the processes of commercial life.

In the following pages the most important

34

President's Advisory Commission on Lamberti
(Spring Outing, Bethesda, Maryland, 1968)

FRONT ROW:
McGeorge Bundy,
Juan Trippe,
John Lindsay,
Thomas J. Watson, Jr.,
Arthur Goldberg,
Archbishop Terence Cooke,
Gene Tunney,
Lionel Trilling,
Alex Rose,
Nathan Pusey,
Paul Newman,
Crawford Greenewalt,
Harry Belafonte,
William McC. Martin.
SECOND ROW:
Same.
THIRD ROW:
Friends of the
Metropolitan Opera
and two men
from NASA.
FOURTH ROW:
Employees of
reputable firms
who have served
more than forty years
and Rhodes Scholars.

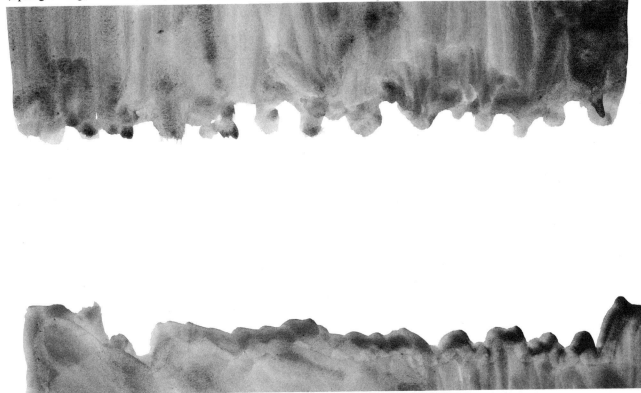

There has never been serious doubt about the xylophone.

The most perceptive analysis to date; both sides presented fairly, with a number of penetrating insights and a firm conclusion, which does not, however, altogether rule out an alternative, or, indeed, several alternatives.

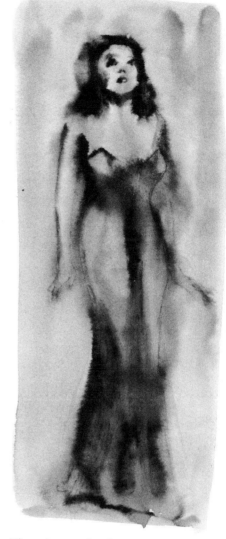

The stripteaser has been authenticated repeatedly. (Above: Margie Hart, from an early photo)

"Lamberti" does not appear in the dictionary. The closest word is:

lam·bert (lăm′bərt), *n.* the cgs unit of brightness;

The addition of the suffix "i" to "Lambert," creating "Lamberti," may have been a blatant attempt to enlist the sympathy of Italians, or those of Italian stock. (This appears to be self-defeating since Italians are basically sympathetic anyway.)

Examples of Reality (Indisputable)

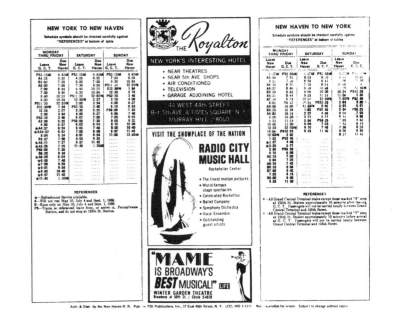

FRANK LESLIE'S ILLUSTRATED NEWSPAPER DECEMBER 1A

Burning of the ferryboat *Idaho*. "A disaster which predicted by those acquainted with the way in which daily was managed has just occurred. The illustrations which accompany will give our readers some idea of the awful scene which was enacted on Monday evening, the 26th of November, by the burning of the ferryboat *Idaho* while crossing from Brooklyn to New York. The excitement which prevailed on both shores while the boat to be seen on fire, and no one knew how many lives were lost by what means those unfortunate persons on board had to escape was terrible to witness. Providentially no lives were lost, but one shudders to think what would have happened, if, instead of only thirty or forty people on board, when the fire broke out, there had been, as is not unusual, between six and eight hundred which number, it may be observed, there would certainly have been when the boat was returning on the same trip from the New York side. It is safe to say that in the horrid confusion that would have arisen, very few would have escaped a miserable death. We may thank God that we have been spared such a catastrophe."—*Frank Leslie's Illustrated Newspaper*, December 15, 1866.

Theodore Roosevelt with lion

Ormond Beach, 1908. Pro-Lamberti forces prize this series of photographs as particularly telling. Anti-Lamberti scholars maintain that the photographs have been "doctored."

The Federal Government's View

A

Will you please
my secretary which date y
may make the necessary a

B

have your secretary advise
you would prefer so that I
arrangements.

Sincerely,

Obviously the same letter
Kick too high, unless Lamberti was an acrobat — no evidence on this.
Note: If there was girl skipper, why not appear in photo? (Indicates that girl did not exist either.)

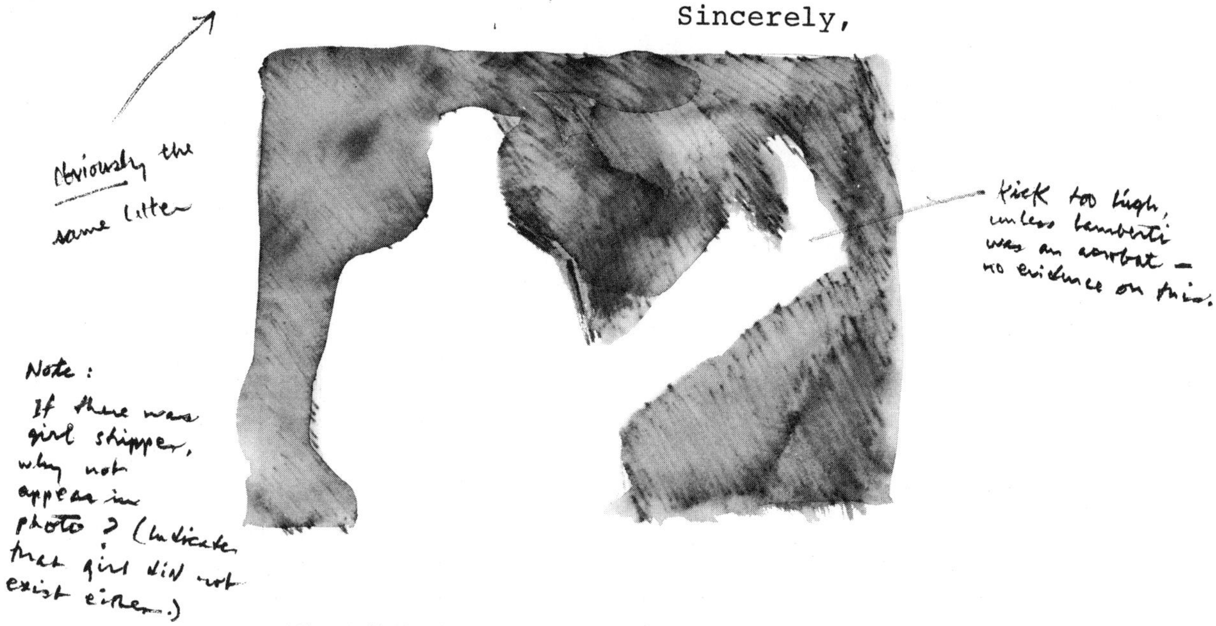

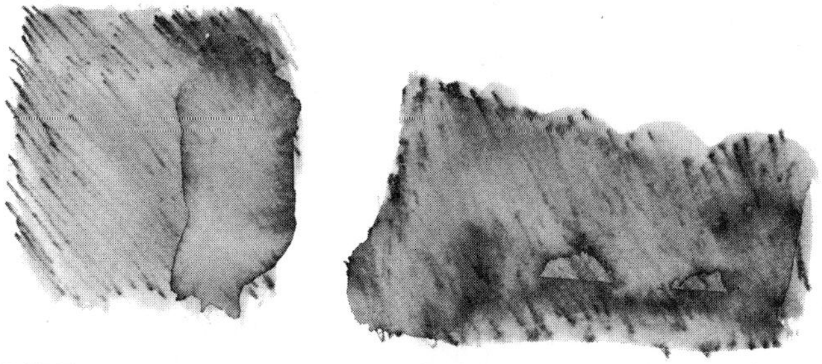

"... considering the evidence, it seems unlikely —in view of the paucity of documentation and the preposterous nature of his 'act'—that Prof. Lamberti ever existed."
Report of the U.S. Bureau of Authentication, 1969

Numerous examples of the Lamberti-type fallacy exist—popular belief sustained by meager documentary evidence in the absence of concrete proof (see illus.).

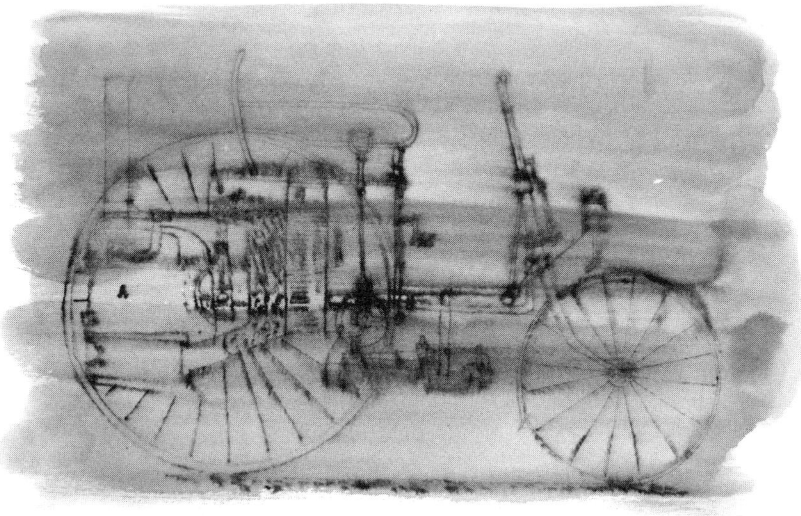

SERPOLLET'S STEAM TRICYCLE.
(FROM MEMORY.)

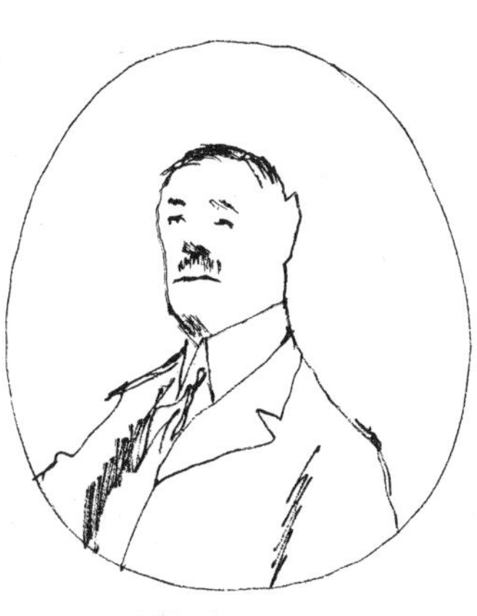

Uncle Ollie from Rochester

An example
of visionary art
produced by
cultists

Aerial View of Franklin Bridge
At Sunset - Photo by King

IF LAMBERTI
WAS NOT REAL I
HAVE NO reason
TO GO on living.
Sincerely,
ED

POST CARD
Address

PLACE
STAMP
HERE

An example of
the most
irresponsible sort of
Lamberti-believer.
*(Note that the card
was never mailed.)*

Proposed Lamberti Memorial
(Early design)

*(Note presence
of R. H. Hendershot,
the original drummer boy
of the Rappahannock—
unfortunately, the
subject of a somewhat
similar cult some years ago.)*

March, Saturday, 2 P.M.–3 P.M.

Two o'clock in the afternoon on the day before Easter. Rain. Rain in the morning, rain now. All the children asleep except Walker. Walker is ten. We go for a walk, down the empty road, around the edges of the puddles. It isn't cold. The heavy sky is pushing down on the soggy grass; at the end of the road, the sea is smoky lavender-gray. We come to where a new house is being built, at the edge of some low woods. The yard is full of lumber; sheets of plywood have turned dark, soaking up the rain. Piles of wood—the sawed-off ends of two-by-fours, trapezoids, kindling—and wet papers in the mud. Beside the house there is a rushing stream; the water plunges into a drain through the openings of a metal cover. There is room to drop things into the drain. Walker finds a white plastic cup; it will serve. Then we will hurry to the sea wall, two hundred yards away, and see if it comes out of the pipe that empties onto the rocks there. Walker drops the cup, and we go over the squishy lawns past the empty houses, through the hedges, across the road. Somewhere beneath us the cup is spinning along, riding in the darkness, heading for the sea—we hope, at least. We cross a final lawn, climb down over the concrete sea wall, and jump over the rocks to where the pipe is—a three-foot hole in the side of the sea wall. It is jammed with rocks, but water is gushing out around them. Walker reaches in and dislodges a boulder; the water bursts out. He pulls away more stones, and now there is a torrent shooting out over the rocks, splattering wildly. It is a horizontal geyser; the water must have been backed up all the way to the swamp in the woods. Sticks and grasses come flying out; the water changes colors. Finally, it subsides to a steady stream. We cannot find the plastic cup. We climb the sea wall again and walk home.

Walker steps in the puddles, watching the water rise over the soles of his loafers. "Don't—you'll get wet feet." He steps onto solid ground and walks along, but is drawn to the next puddle, and his loafers move through it, leading a life of their own. We reach our house and open the door slowly—it squeaks. We are afraid it will wake the others. "Let's oil the door." We start a search for an oilcan. The bottom drawer in the

kitchen: no. Out into the garage. Two drawers in a workbench: no. A closet: no. We cross the driveway to Grandma's house (empty for the winter) and enter her garage.

An old-fashioned oilcan, the sort a railroad engineer carries in pictures, sits on a beam. We try it—*clunk; clonk*. It is rusty and empty. Into a small room where the water pump stands. The pump is oily and silent. THE F. E. MYERS & BRO. CO., ASHLAND, OHIO, it says on one side, and on the other side there is an emblem: TAKE OFF YOUR HAT TO THE MYERS . . . PUMPS FOR EVERY PURPOSE . . . HAY TOOLS & DOOR HANGERS. Nearby are paint cans, a wheelbarrow, glass jars of nails, weed killer, turpentine. Over the doorway on a two-by-four is a key; reach up and fumble in the dust. The fingers find the key and its bit of string and its tag.

We leave the garage and go to the back door of Grandma's house and un-

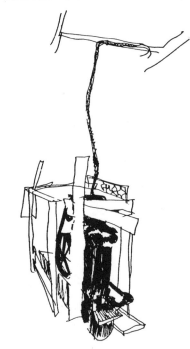

lock it. We enter the house. A closet near the kitchen: a shelf of cleaning fluids, soaps, spot removers, ant buttons. We close the door again and try a closet in the back hall. It is locked. We go through the dining room to Grandma's desk, unlock and open the lid, pull out a drawer, and find the key marked CLOSET. Take the key, return to the hall, unlock the closet, open the door; a white can sits on a shelf, waiting. 3-IN-ONE OIL, it says. It looks new, it looks full; we grab

it and go. Out the door, across the driveway, around to the front door. Walker opens it slowly, but it cries out anyway. I reach up and oil the hinges. Walker lets go, the door gives the faintest start of a groan, then slides silently shut. We open it again—no sound. We let it close: utter silence. We tiptoe through the house, testing every door—old wooden ones on ancient hinges, new ones, the swinging doors in the kitchen—dispensing oil to each. Even the ones that don't need it; they might need it someday.

The downstairs now is steeped in silence. Doors, one after the other, swing out and back, demonstrating their quietude. We oil the hinges on the top of the deep freeze, finally, and then the house is done.

We carry the oilcan back to Grandma's house, and put it on the shelf of the closet in the back hall. Close the closet door. Lock it. Remove the key. Put the key back in the desk drawer, close the drawer, then close the desk. We walk back through the empty house and out. Close the door. It locks itself. We take the key out and go into the garage and put the key back on the two-by-four over the door. Then we leave the garage, close the door, and walk across the shiny gravel to our house. The rain is coming down. Behind us, four hundred yards along the sea wall, the water is streaming from the swamp, through the pipe under the lawns, and out onto the rocks and over them into the sea. (Is the white plastic cup out there now, riding on the cold gray waves?) In the house, downstairs, no doors squeak. We part. Walker goes up the stairs to his room to read; I go into the living room. We separate without saying goodbye. Everyone is still asleep upstairs.

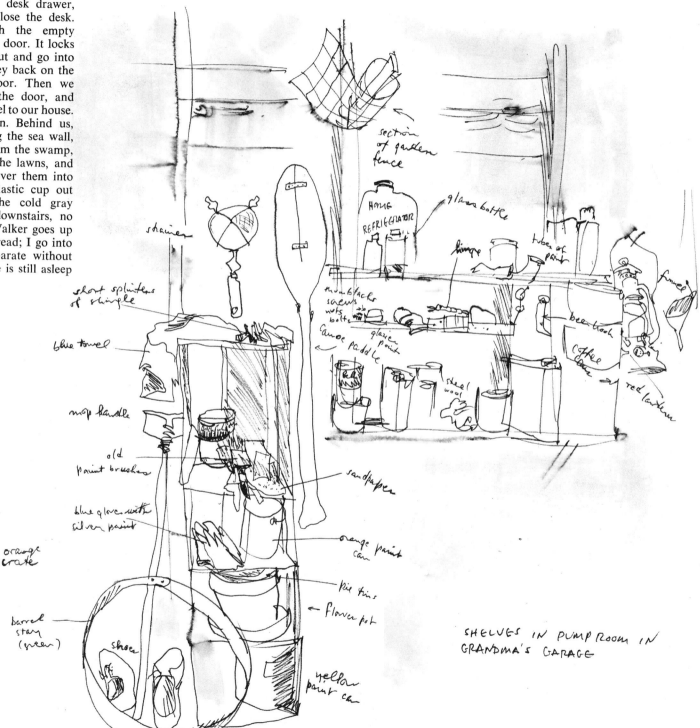

section of garden fence

HOME REFRIGERATOR

glass bottle

shaver

hinge

tube of paint

funnel

beer flask

Coffee can

red lantern

short splinters of shingle

thumbtacks screws nuts bolts

glazier point

canoe paddle

steel wool

blue towel

mop handle

old paint brushes

sandpaper

blue gloves with silver paint

orange paint can

orange crate

pie tins

flower pot

barrel stay (green)

shoes

yellow paint can

SHELVES IN PUMP ROOM IN GRANDMA'S GARAGE

The Last Days of...

TOOTIE 'N' FRED

But Recently—

LIBERTY FEATURES
SYNDICATE
N. ████████, Chicago Ill

Nov. ░ ░░░

Mr. 'Spud' Willis
9477 Desencahtada Blvd.
Los Angeles ███, ████████.

Dear 'spud':
   What's the matter kid?
50 Years in the business
Yours has ALWAYS be-
en one of the GREAT
strips! AMERICA loves
"TOOTIE & FRED"
Christ 800 PAPERS
KID!!!

What I am getting at
'spud' is --- your Most
*Recent strips HAVE
FRANKLY LACKED
PiZZAZZ. Let's go, 'spud..!
          Warmest regards
          Sincerely,
          Jim
          Executive Vice President

P.S. 93 papers
have canceled.
(No cause for alarm. Probably
seasonal.)

← WAS THIS
LETTER

JUSTIFIED?

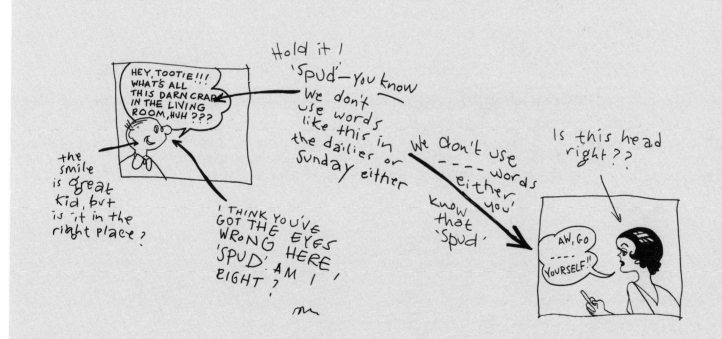

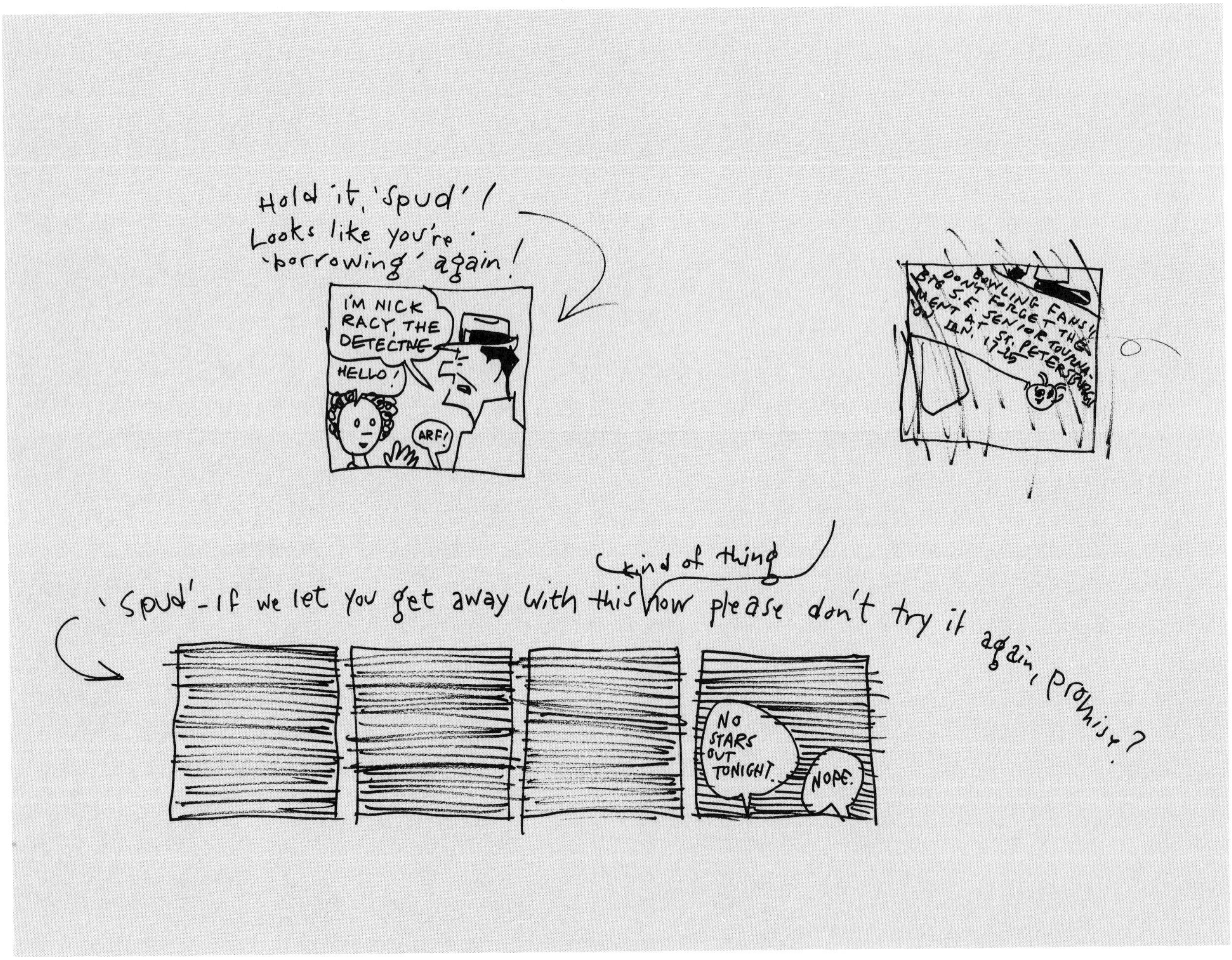

Hold it, 'spud'!
Looks like you're 'borrowing' again!
I'M NICK RACY, THE DETECTIVE
HELLO!
ARF!
BOWLING FANS!! DON'T FORGET THE BIG S.E. SENIOR TOURNAMENT AT ST. PETERSBURG! ON JAN. 17-25
'spud' - if we let you get away with this kind of thing now please don't try it again, promise?
NO STARS OUT TONIGHT.
NOPE.

Is this the most effective use of space, kid?
i.e. 'Spvd'-- can you work a little bigger in future?

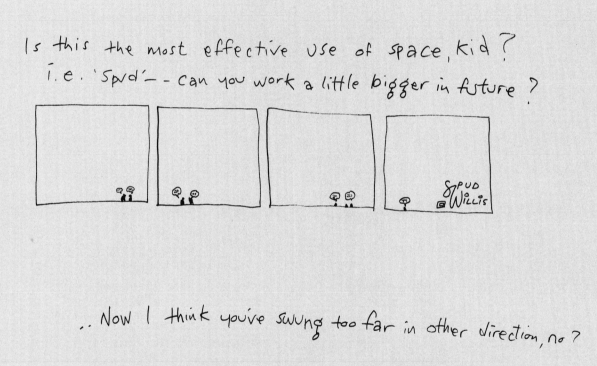

.. Now I think you've swung too far in other direction, no?

This has some of the OLD VITALITY but
-- The story line seems weak here, 'Spud.'

The face keeps changing, no?

(should his suit
be black?)

please, Spud
OH, SHIT!!
SPUD WILLIS
Isn't one cowlick sufficient?
Looks like you're copying Ben Day again, pal — Why?

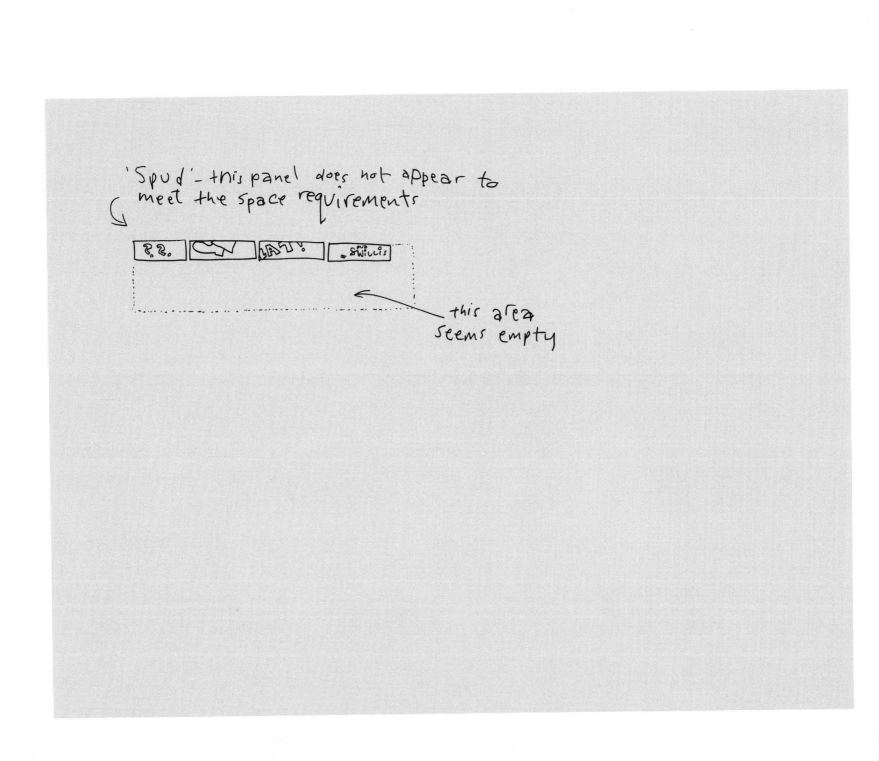

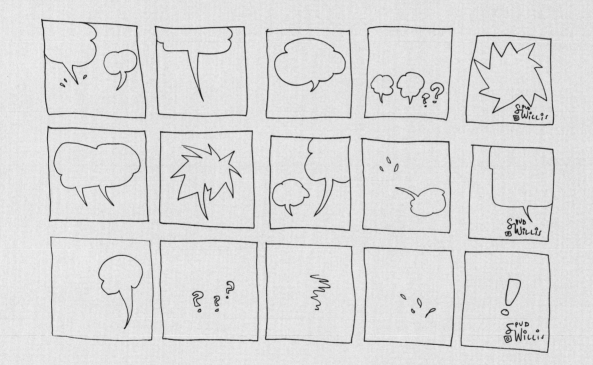

We can't regard these as 'finished' work as defined in yr. contract,
'spud' ——

'Spud'---Let's not forget that comics are essentially VISUAL.
Also, looks like you are having 'story' problems again.

TOOTIE 'N' FRED

HEAT FOUR SERVICE PLATES AND CENTER EACH WITH A STUFFED BAKED POTATO SLASHED AND DRESSED WITH A BIT OF BUTTER AND DASH OF PAPRIKA. ARRANGE AROUND THE POTATO A PORTION OF BUTTERED WAX BEANS, CORN AND SQUASH SAUTÉ AND SPINACH. BESIDE THE SPINACH PLACE A LETTUCE CUP CONTAINING A TABLE-SPOON OF HEATED RUSSIAN DRESSING. GARNISH WITH

PARSLEY OR RADISHES CARRYING A TUFT OF GREEN LEAVES. TO PREPARE THE RUSSIAN DRESSING WHICH LIFTS THE SPINACH FROM THE COMMONPLACE THE FOLLOWING RECIPE MAY PROVE HELPFUL.

RUSSIAN DRESSING

ONE-HALF CUP MAYONNAISE (BOUGHT)
FOUR TABLESPOONS CHILI SAUCE, OR MORE
ONE-HALF TABLESPOON FINGLY MINCED PEPPER OR INDIA RELISH
YIELD: THREE-FOURTHS CUP.
FOLD CHILI SAUCE AND MINCED PEPPER OR RELISH

INTO MAYONNAISE. SET BOWL IN LARGER BOWL CONTAINING HOT WATER; STIR UNTIL HEATED SLIGHTLY; SERVE IN LETTUCE CUPS WITH THE SPINACH.

SPUD Willis

Reg. U.S. Pat. Off. Copyright by Roberts Features Inc.

(One of the gang at the office tells me this was 'cribbed' from a '32 Daily News, 'Spud.' Say it ain't so...)

The Last Panel Received from Spud Willis

View From the Log

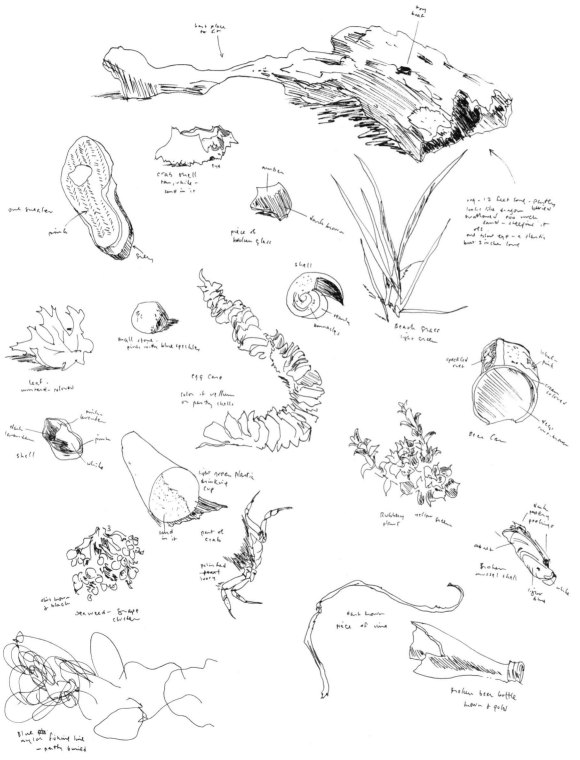

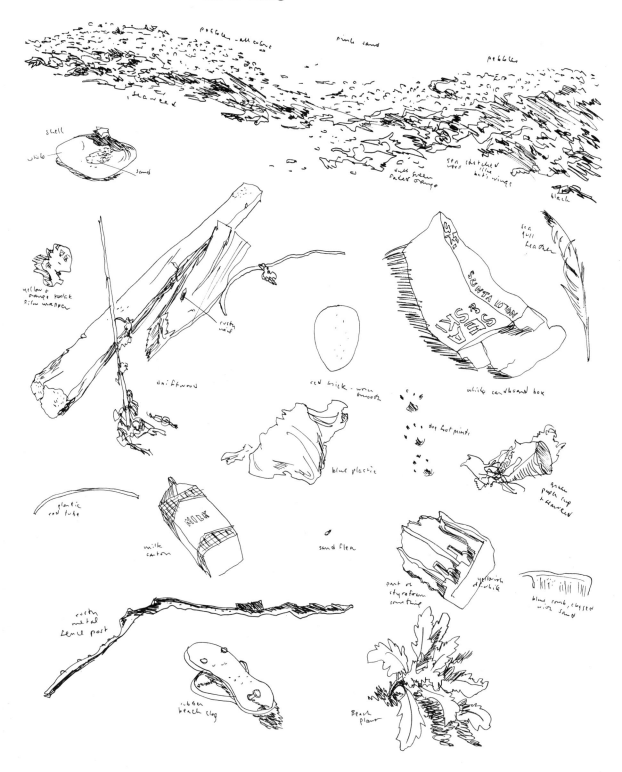

near the water

pebbles - all colors

pink sand

pebbles

seaweed

shell

white

sand

dull green
faded orange

sea stretches
like
bird's wings

black

yellow &
orange kodak
film wrapper

driftwood

rusty
nail

red brick - worn
smooth

dog bat mints

sea
gull
feather

SUNTAN LOTION

ALASKA

white cardboard box

green
paper cup
+ seaweed

plastic
red tube

MILK

blue plastic

sand flea

milk
carton

part of
styrofoam
something

yellowish
off white

blue comb, clogged
with sand

rusty
metal
fence post

rubber
beach clog

beach
plant

Beat the Doldrums
(Make your summer a meaningful experience)

Don Heckman and His Tub
Heckman, a serious man, approaches his tub-rolling exercises in a solemn manner. "If you want to do it right, you can't kid around," he says. Sensitive to criticism that he is fun loving, Heckman explains, "There is no 'fun' in the tub-rolling whatsoever."

Step 1. Saying hello to the tub.

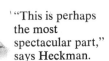

"This is perhaps the most spectacular part," says Heckman.

Defenestration at the Union Club
Everett Toomey, Jr., enlivens afternoons at the Union Club by inviting old friends for a drink on the fourth floor. When his companions begin to lament the state of the market, Toomey exclaims, "By George, you're right!" and jumps out the window. (Roberts, the doorman, and Phelps, the cue-chalker, wait on the sidewalk with a fireman's net.)

"Let Me Do It"

Frederick M. Dunlop, of Rye, N.Y., is a skillful carver. On Saturday nights during the summer, he roams the Rye-Purchase area—sometimes venturing as far as Greenwich—carrying his knife and fork, knocking on doors at dinner time, and inquiring of residents whether they'd like him to carve. Fred never lingers; he does the job briskly, then goes on his way.

At the Hazletts'

At the Browns'

At the Gummerles'

At the Fosters'

At the Martin-Smyths'

At the Derbys'

At the Camerons'

At the Huntingtons'

At the Barnams'

At the Chases'

At the Woolmans'

At the Barrises'

Flagpole Frolic
Charlie Noonan was dismayed when the vest he had ordered from Brooks Brothers arrived with a built-in flagpole, but he quickly turned the mistake into a "plus." (Right: Noonan and Al, the TV repairman.)

Family Fun—Bloomington, Ind.
Lars Nilsson arranges his large family in unusual and attractive patterns to surprise guests.

RICK

The Waterfall "Stunt"
Ogden M. Cole (dark suit, left), of Ausable Chasm, N.Y., invites friends to dress up, go on a picnic, then pose for a photograph under Hickley's Bluff (right). Ogden's brother, Rick, stationed above, waits till guests are posed, then pours water on them. Ladies at right outsmarted Cole; they had their "picture taken" last year.

Pleasure Beach

Band concert, 1909

View from water, July 4, 1946

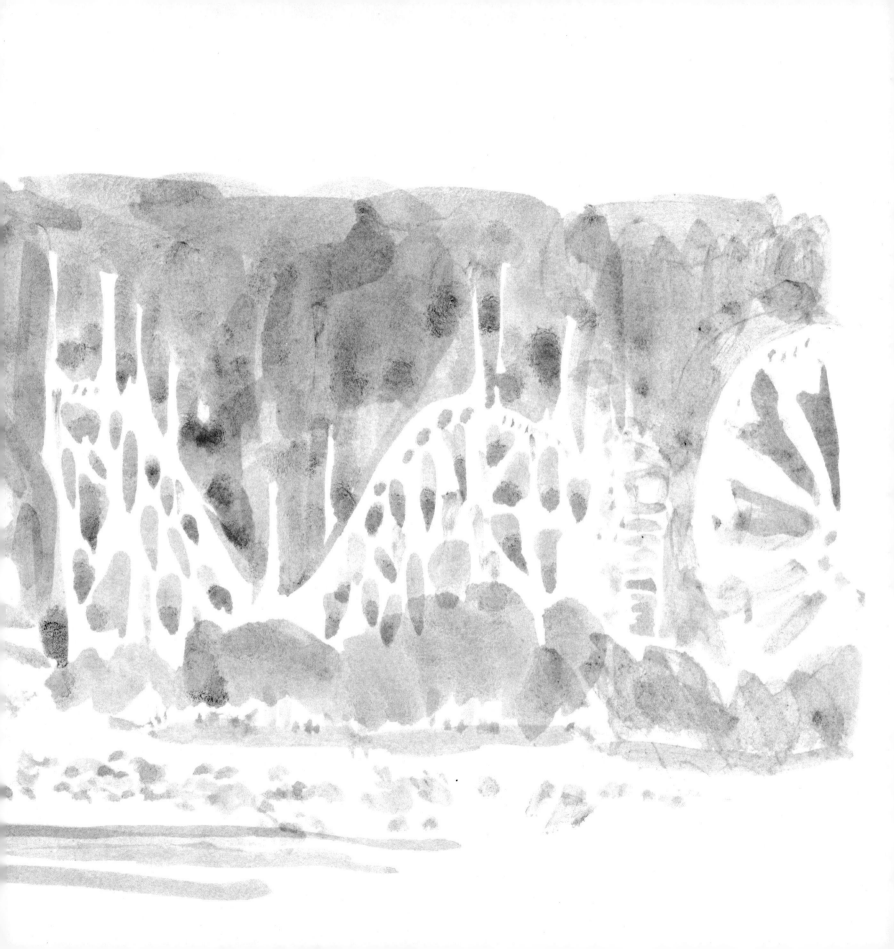

Trolley arriving at Bay Avenue entrance, 1901

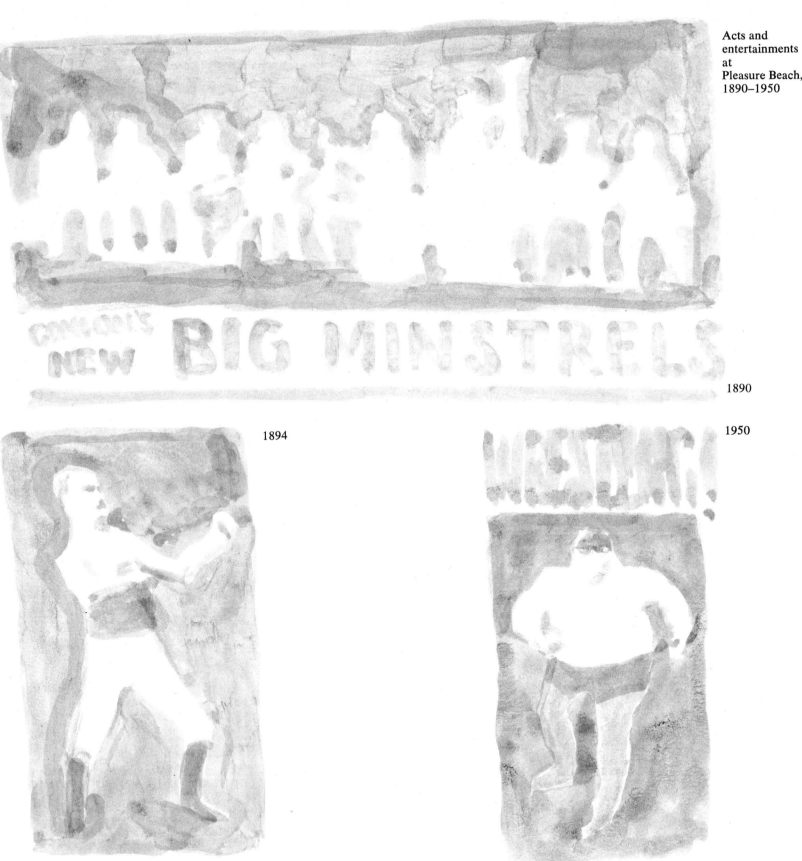

Acts and
entertainments
at
Pleasure Beach,
1890–1950

1890

1894

1950

1905

WILD WEST

1939

1900

1910

Hotel Excelsior Bar, 1935
(third longest bar on East Coast)

Mayor Mahoney (left) visits the boardwalk, 1936.   J. H. (Big John) Rizzuto is host.

The Serpent, 1936

Bicycle club outing, 1890

Guests arriving Hotel Bellair, 1940

Pollock's World's Museum, 1903

Postcard, 1924

Demonstration of airplane over beach, 1911

Gubernatorial campaign, 1906

The pier (destroyed in '38 hurricane)

Verne "Trigger" Atkins—
apprehended after
gun battle on the pier, 1932

Al Carl and His Cosmopolitans
(dance marathon on pier, 1934)

Flagpole sitter, 1929

Sally Costello and Seaman First Class Lou Santoni
in take-your-own-picture booth, the pier (1943)

Starlight Lounge, 1945

SENSATIONAL!
Vicky
VICTORY
2 SHOWS NITELY

Excursion from pier
to Lone Tree Island, 1895

Van's "Beach" Theatre,
Beach St., 1911
(formerly Allen's Variety Hall)

Pleasure Beach, 1969
(Interstate 75)

Why I Am an Unsuccessful Artist

One of the questions I am asked most frequently is "Why are you an unsuccessful artist?" (The other questions are "What time is it?," "Is this the way to the railroad station?," and "Where is my money?") The answer is perfectly simple.

Reason 1 (Winter): Between my house and my studio (see MAP) there are patches of ice beneath the snow. No matter how cautiously I walk, carrying my cup of coffee with great care so as not to spill a drop, there comes a moment when, unfortunately, I realize that once again I have stepped upon the ice. My feet fly out; I yell;[1] I land on my back, and lie gazing at the sky as a shower of hot coffee rains down upon me. Slowly, painfully, I right myself and crawl back to my house through the cold snow.

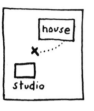

MAP

[1] Slipping-on-ice-yell:

Reason 2: My paintings are too large—generally twenty feet by forty feet, or thereabouts (see EXAMPLE A). In order to display a painting, I need a minimum of four people who are willing to stand—with their shoes off, preferably—at the four corners of the canvas. In the early stages of unrolling, I require only two barefooted volunteers, but two more must be ready to jump onto their corners at the instant the entire canvas is unrolled—and quickly, too. Otherwise, the whole thing may shoot back like a window blind, rolling me up in it. So the four volunteers must be: (1) available; (2) willing to take off their shoes; (3) blessed with pleasant personalities, so that they will get along with one another; (4) discreet, and not make smart comments about my painting as it is slowly revealed; and (5) agile. (A corollary reason that could be appended here is *Impatient Art Dealers.* They are often brisk and are apt to say, "Thank you, I have seen enough," when I have only begun to unroll my canvas. One dismissed me after only two and a half feet.[2]) Also, the volunteers should be heavy. I have tried using children, but they sometimes sail right across the room.[3] Dogs, I find, are unreliable.

EXAMPLE A
LARGE PAINTING

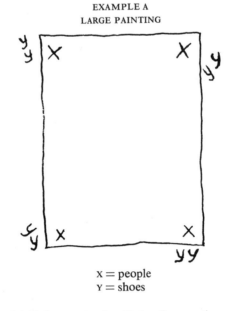

x = people
y = shoes

[2] Aside from my own humiliation, there was the embarrassment of having to apologize to my four volunteers, who glared at me as they began to put their shoes back on, thinking of the long trip back to the country. Two of them did not even get to stand on their corners. We had to stop at Howard Johnson's on the way home.

[3] They love this, but it is distracting; it should be reserved for birthdays only.

Reason 3: My small paintings are too small. When people say that my large paintings are too large, I attempt to oblige by "working small." Inevitably, the comment comes that these paintings (see EXAMPLE B) are "too" small. Potential patrons complain that it is difficult to incorporate my small paintings into their general scheme of decoration,[4] and also that when they wish to show my paintings to visitors much time is consumed in locating them, owing to their size.

Reason 4: Philosophy. I firmly believe: (*a*) utter despair is just around the corner, and (*b*) something really marvelous is about to happen. Holding such divergent views simultaneously makes my hand shake and my paintbrush tremble, and I get turpentine on my city shoes.

Reason 5: More philosophy. In my view, nothing in life is ever complete (except death), so I rarely finish anyth

EXAMPLE B
(Enlarged 100 times)

[4] Obtaining attractive frames is especially difficult.

Oberfest

. . . Through scenery of surpassing loveliness, we descend into the tranquil valley, and make our way to the ancient, fortified town of Oberfest. The origin of the old town is veiled in the poetic darkness of tradition. For many centuries, it has ruled itself, and coined its own monies. Entering the square, the Town Hall is admirably brought before the eye. It is the very embodiment of grandeur and sublimity: a colossal, many-towered, complex structure, aspiring toward heaven, with countless gables and spires, turrets, and gilded cupolas. One is compelled to venerate the simple townsfolk whose stern virtue and zeal have enabled them to oppose the incursions of those who would conquer, yet have made of their town a repository of all that is grand in antiquity, and ceaselessly striven to beautify and adorn, to elevate and refine. . . . Rising above the sunlit pinnacles of the Hall loom mountains of extraordinary steepness, and awesome, savage magnificence. In winter, it is said, fearful avalanches roll down from these heights.—A Traveller in Europe, by G. Brown, F.B.S., with Numerous Wood Engravings, by the Best Artists, 1871.

On a morning in early spring, 1873, the people of Oberfest left their houses and took refuge in the town hall. No one knows why, precisely. A number of rumors had raced through the town during recent weeks, and there was a profound uneasiness among the people. Idle talk and gossip was passed on and converted to news; predictions became certainties. On this particular morning, fear turned into terror, and people rushed through the narrow streets, carrying their most precious possessions, pulling their children, and dashed into the great hall. The first to arrive occupied the largest rooms; the others found space in smaller rooms, in hallways, on stairs, in the towers. The doors were nailed shut, and men took turns watching out the windows. Two days passed. Order was maintained. The unruly, the sick, and the unstable were consigned to the cellars; the cellar stairs were guarded. When no disaster came, the fear grew worse because the people began to suspect that the danger was already within the hall, locked inside. No one spoke to anybody else; people watched each other, looking for signs. It was the children who rang the great bell in the first bell tower—a small band of bored children, unable to bear the silence and having run through all the halls, slid down all the banisters, climbed all the turrets. They found the bell rope and swung on it—set the bell clanging. This was the traditional signal of alarm, and in a moment the elders were dashing in panic to all the other bell towers, and ringing the bells. For nearly an hour, the valley reverberated with the wild clangor— and then, a thousand feet above, the snow began to crack, and the avalanche began; a massive cataract of ice and snow thundered down and buried the town, silencing the bells. There is no trace of Oberfest today, not even a spire, because the snow is so deep; and, in the shadow of the mountains, it is very cold.

Goodhue: Forgotten Hero of American Science and Technology

This year marks the 150th anniversary of the birth of Eleazar Goodhue (1820–1910), pioneer inventor and scientific wizard

Goodhue

Bad Day at High Bridge: Simultaneous failure of the Goodhue automatic railroad safety switch, the Goodhue superior friction brake, and the Goodhue steer-right rudder

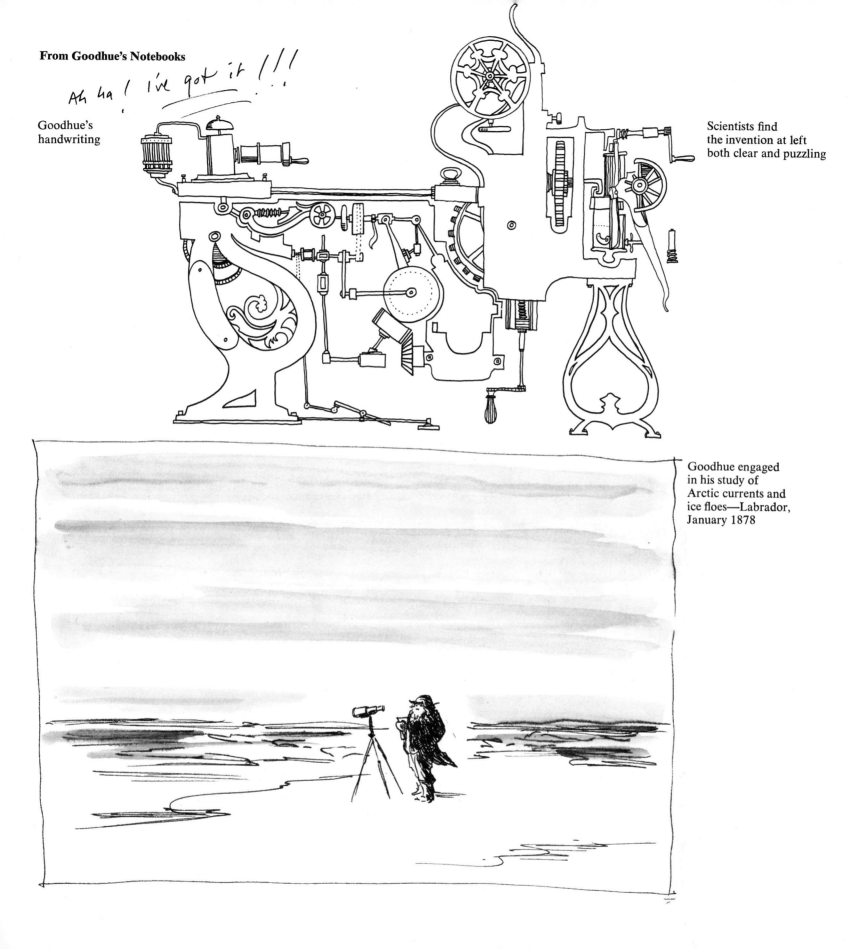

From Goodhue's Notebooks

Ah ha! I've got it!!!

Goodhue's
handwriting

Scientists find
the invention at left
both clear and puzzling

Goodhue engaged
in his study of
Arctic currents and
ice floes—Labrador,
January 1878

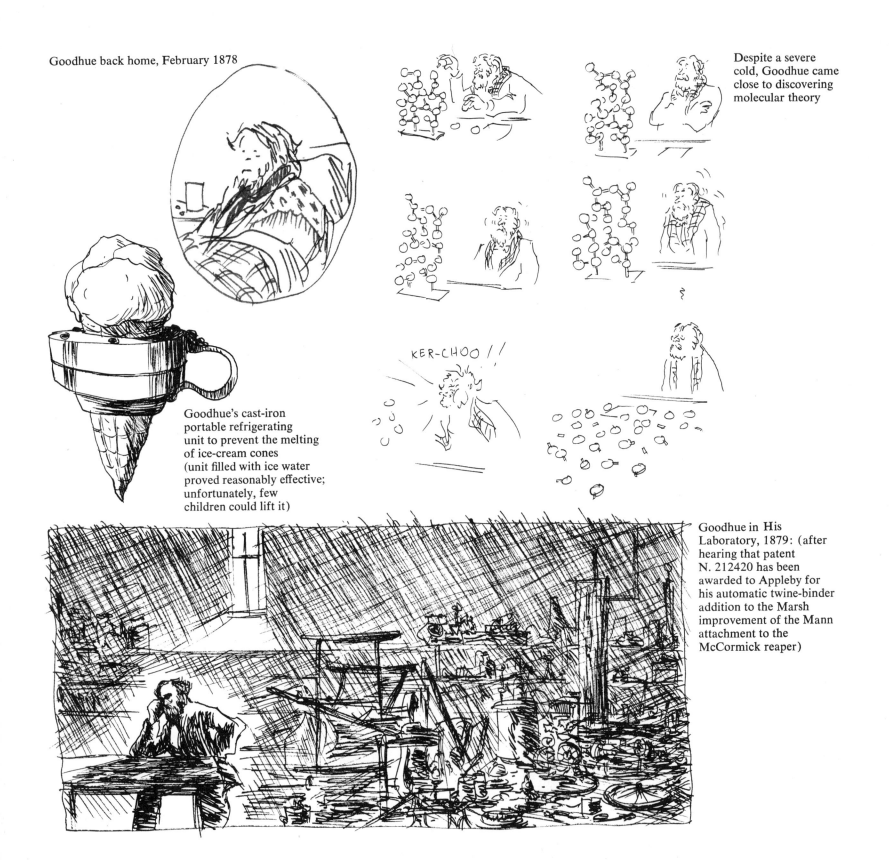

Goodhue back home, February 1878

Despite a severe cold, Goodhue came close to discovering molecular theory

KER-CHOO!!

Goodhue's cast-iron portable refrigerating unit to prevent the melting of ice-cream cones (unit filled with ice water proved reasonably effective; unfortunately, few children could lift it)

Goodhue in His Laboratory, 1879: (after hearing that patent N. 212420 has been awarded to Appleby for his automatic twine-binder addition to the Marsh improvement of the Mann attachment to the McCormick reaper)

Goodhue Investigates the Cantilever Principle

Placing the weight, Goodhue . . .

descends . . .

examines his experiment (note bird [upper right])

. . . apparent success! (bird lands an instant later)

Goodhue's Pioneering Often Cost Him

His prototype safety razor

Goodhue and his sewing machine (note fingers)

Carelessness caused
Goodhue to miss out on
the first successful
telephone transmission
(note frog pond at right)

The First Day   9 A.M.   10 A.M.   11 A.M.   11:05 A.M.

Goodhue was a loner. His collaboration with Meissenauer, the great German chemist, was short-lived.

On the Rocky Shore of Lake Huron The First (and Last) Flight

Goodhue and his glider (note rock)

Goodhue inadvertently separated from glider

Glider on its way toward Canada

How Goodhue Almost Beat Edison

Although it never
actually flew,
Goodhue's 1909 airplane
embodied a bold innovation—
the concept of "six across"

Goodhue was
very nearly first
with a successful
vacuum tube

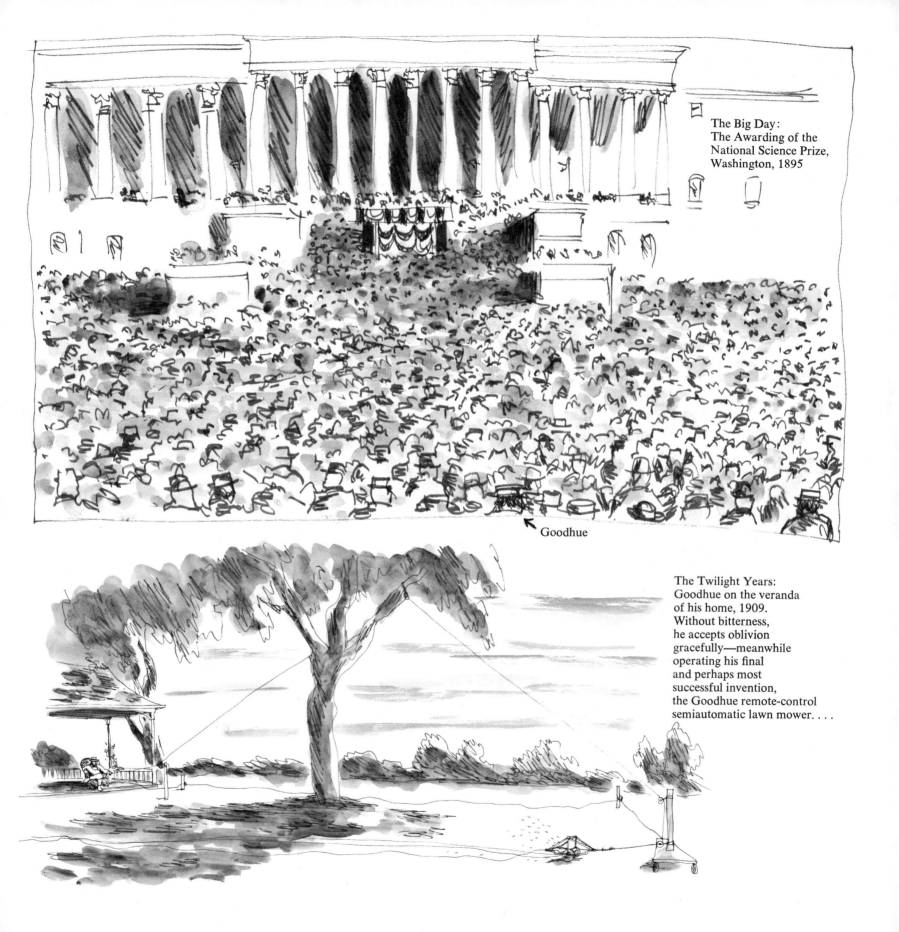

The Big Day:
The Awarding of the
National Science Prize,
Washington, 1895

Goodhue

The Twilight Years:
Goodhue on the veranda
of his home, 1909.
Without bitterness,
he accepts oblivion
gracefully—meanwhile
operating his final
and perhaps most
successful invention,
the Goodhue remote-control
semiautomatic lawn mower. . . .

What To Do on a Saturday

Think about Grandpa (He was a kind man.)

Plant a morning glory

Weigh yourself

Take your sweetie for a spin

Send a card to a friend

POST CARD

HOW YA DOIN' PAL ?!?

Regards,
Ralph

Buy a pineapple

Look out the window at the kite string lying on the lawn

Take a pill

Do some reading

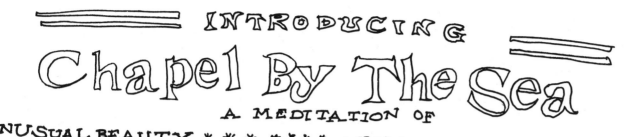

Try a new tune on your mandolin

The Pianoforte Factory Revisited

A QUESTION:

Those of us who recall with deep nostalgic pleasure the charming if somewhat tedious essay, "A Day at a Pianoforte Factory," from the 1848 *Guide to Knowledge*[1] may ask ourselves from time to time, "What has happened to the old pianoforte factory in the intervening one hundred and twenty-two years?"

WHAT HAS HAPPENED TO THE OLD PIANOFORTE FACTORY IN THE INTERVENING ONE HUNDRED AND TWENTY-TWO YEARS:

The pianoforte factory is not what it used to be. There are cobwebs everywhere, and transistor radios turned too loud; everyone listens to a different station. Morale is terrible. Fret-cutters are impossible to find. They can get more money elsewhere. Ed, the last remaining fret-cutter, mumbles to himself. He is thinking of getting a job as a digital-computer operator. It would mean working in a nice, clean, sunny place. "Simple systems tend to be linear," Ed whispers to himself, "with only one feedback loop." He cuts a fret, then adds, "Complex systems are nonlinear and involve many feedback loops." Ed will be leaving soon.[2]

TESTING THE INSTRUMENTS:

Once a year, in September, MacNamee & Uzzle come to the pianoforte factory to select new pianos. MacNamee & Uzzle are the famous piano team, whose keyboard artistry is so popular. The team moves quietly through the dim factory. (One member of the team is very strange, while the other man only pretends to be strange, so as not to call attention to the first. Since it is difficult to remember which one is authentically peculiar, people in the pianoforte factory treat both men with caution.) Now the manager of the factory shows the team the new pianos, dusting the stools for them with a silk handkerchief. Soon the air is filled with the famous four-hand arrangement of "Frenesi." Suddenly, MacNamee stops. "No, no, no!" he cries. He kicks the pedals. "You call this piece of junk a pianoforte?" he demands. He knocks over his stool. (MacNamee may very well be the peculiar one.) "What do you think, Uzzle?" he asks.

Uzzle looks thoughtful. "Speak . . . more . . . slowly," he says. (In times of stress, Uzzle pretends not to understand English.[3]) They move on to the next pair of pianos. The manager smiles privately. Although the team does not know this, the manager is not showing them the very finest pianos in stock. This is because they have not yet paid for the last pair of pianos.

HOSTILITY AMONG EMPLOYEES:

Deirdre, a real looker, is new in hammer-felting, yet her picture has appeared a number of times in *Arpeggio*, the house organ. Some of the ladies in hammer-felting have been keeping a record of which pictures appear in *Arpeggio*, and how often. This is the score (through Labor Day):

STAFF CHANGES:

Marsden, who was in charge of Public Relations and Community Affairs, has been replaced by a three-man committee. Marsden, a squat, morose man, is thought to have done little for the company image during his twenty-seven years at the factory. Some think that he lacked the delicate sensitivity needed for this type of work, what with his natural reluctance to be pleasant, apologetic, or civil. Marsden's last months at the factory were spent largely in leaning out his third-floor window and hailing passersby below. Upon catching their attention, he would then leer, and categorize them in a loud, mocking voice. ("Weirdo" was one of his favorite appellations; also "Freak," "Yo-Yo," and "Creep.") This name-calling, especially when paired with sweeping, vulgar gestures, undoubtedly cost the company something in good will.

EXAMINATION AND TUNING ROOM:

The final room in the pianoforte factory is the Examination and Tuning Room. There, every instrument is carefully checked. The key-counter counts the keys, and if there are not *precisely* eighty-eight, the instrument is rejected, and sent back through the factory for a completely new keyboard. "Here comes another goddamn

1. Interior of a Pianoforte Factory   2. Fret-cutter at work

3. The "Action," or Internal Mechanism, of a Cabinet Pianoforte

eighty-seven!" yells Herb, the burly key-counter, giving a piano a terrific shove. The piano rumbles back through the building, screeching along on its casters until it reaches the Keyboard Department. Here George, the keyboard man, glares at the instrument as it strikes the wall. He is surly and approaching retirement age,[4] and refuses to believe he has erred. With one finger he counts the keys: "One, two, three, four . . ." When he reaches eighty-seven, and there are no more keys, he merely shrugs. "Big deal," he snarls. "Only fruits use that top key, anyway."

The tuner for the pianoforte factory is Mr. Faber. He is a neat, scholarly looking man with a small mustache, and a flower in his buttonhole. He comes in on Wednesdays. He stands in the doorway, pulling off his gloves and gazing at the gleaming new pianos. He speaks to no one; he seems to be whistling quietly. He *is* whistling quietly, in fact. At home, just before leaving for the pianoforte factory, Mr. Faber follows a rigid routine. He dresses, then steps over to his piano and strikes middle C. He whistles the note, then strikes the C again, to confirm that he is whistling the precise note. Then he takes a huge breath, hits C, whistles it, and races out the door and down the street, and takes the bus to the pianoforte factory, softly whistling C all the way. Once he has tuned middle C on the first piano of the day to the precise pitch of his whistled C, he stops whistling, and is able to relax.[5] (A sad sidelight to this is that Faber has lost confidence in recent years, and has come to believe that he is whistling D flat en route to the factory, or B sharp. Thus, on Wednesdays, one can now see Faber dart out of his house, run down the sidewalk, skid to a stop, run back to his house, and dash in. Then—a moment later—he comes flying out again, hurtles down the street, stops, goes running back, etc., over and over again. It makes the neighbors terribly nervous, and sometimes Faber does not actually reach the factory until four in the afternoon.)

1 *The Guide to Knowledge, or Repertory of Facts; Forming a Complete Library of Entertaining Information in the Several Departments of Science, Literature, and Art.* Embellished by Several Hundred Engravings.* Edited by Robert Sears. Twelfth Edition. New York: Edward Walker, 114 Fulton Street. MDCCCXLVIII. (Needs dusting.)

*See Illustrations 1, 2, 3.

2 The strange thing is that Ed used to dream of becoming a fret-cutter, believing that once he was cutting frets on a full-time basis then everything would be all right.

3 On second thought, perhaps Uzzle is the strange one.

4 He is disturbed by the thought of retiring, since his heart is in keyboards. "What the hell am I gonna *do*?" he demands suddenly, often directing the question at whoever is nearby. They do not know what he is talking about. (He should seek professional help.)

5 It is curious that Faber does not use a tuning fork, but the truth is that Faber lost his tuning fork some years ago, possibly at the company picnic in 1949, which was voted the best outing ever by the whole gang. See Illustration 4.

4. 1952 Outing (Not as much fun as 1949)

Waiting for Wingfield

" In the summer of 1873 the guests at an English house party near London were entertained by

from a drawing after an engraving after a photograph in the Illus. Sporting and Dramatic News, London. July 31, 1875.

Major Walter C. Wingfield

of the BRITISH ARMY

who taught them a new lawn game

which he considered

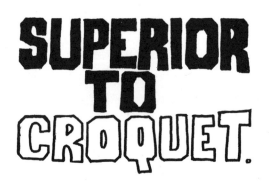

SUPERIOR TO CROQUET.

—From *The Pageant of America*, 1929

Lawn Games and House Party Activities, Tried on Saturday Morning Prior to the Arrival of Wingfield, Which Did Not "Catch On."

Members of the house party moments before arrival of Major Wingfield

When asked to perform his celebrated leap over the tea table, Sir Lawrence readily assented.

For the first time in his life he missed, and destroyed a set of Staffordshire, which, the hostess explained, was of no great value— although of enormous sentimental importance to her family.

H. Farrington withdrew from group activities entirely and spent the day painting a ruin on the estate next door (a rebuke to his host, whose own ruin was several centuries older).

Baron Strüssendorf came prepared with a game *he* thought superior to croquet, but it was so complex that no one could understand the rules.

"...WENN ALLE SCHÖN BRAV WAREN UND SICH NICHT ZU LAUT ZANKTEN, ERHALTEN SIE AM SCHLUSS EINE KLEINE BELOHNUNG!*"

*IF THEY ALL BEHAVE NICELY AND DO NOT QUARREL TOO LOUDLY THEY ARE GIVEN A SMALL TREAT AT THE END.

"*Mens sana in corpore sano!*" said Otto von Weber with a chuckle. "Here is something you will laugh and enjoy. *Follow me!*" He began some simple exercises from the gymnasium, chanting, "*Frisch, fröhlich, und frei . . .*" No one followed. "So you wish to humiliate me?" he cried. Then he smiled abruptly. "It is interesting that Metternich suppressed the *Turnverein*," he said, sitting on the ground and wiping his brow. "Ah, but it is stupid, this nonsense from the *Turnplatz . . .* I myself was never a member."

Those who took a stroll near the arboretum were likely to encounter Honoré Ouillet, who stepped out from behind a tree, with a pair of épées and a cry of

En garde!

. . . no one wanted anything to do with him,

TIENS...

so he hid again behind the tree.

11:15 A.M.

11:45 A.M.

11:50 A.M.

The Duke, as usual, thought it might be amusing if everybody "dressed up." He did, but no one else did. (This did not dampen his spirits, however, and he changed costume three times before noon.)

In the midmorning heel-and-toe race, Sir Thomas G. Cowdrey outdistanced everyone, partly because he yelled, "On your marks, ready, set, *go!*" and began while the others were still discussing whether or not to have a race. Sir Thomas crossed the moor in 1:17.53, and when he came to the railroad station, he boarded the 11:23 and was not seen again.

Others tried their hand at translating the "Kinos Monolith" (which had been discovered by Sir Bernard near the famous "falling palace," in a pile of debris discarded by Schliemann. It remains untranslated to this day, but is available to scholars; Sir Bernard keeps it in the trunk of his Hispano-Suiza. Sir Bernard had planned to reconstruct the entire palace of Kinos but had lost interest halfway through the mosaic floor of the throne room. "Bloody awful lot of little pieces, what?" he said, and abandoned the project.).

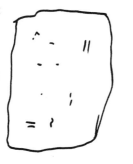

Several guests tried a ride on the skiff Velocipede, but no one enjoyed it very much, except Fred Rivers, from Ohio, U.S.A. (cousin of the host), who took two turns.

Archery caught on briefly with some of the ladies but failed as a group activity, since no men could be persuaded to enter the area.

An early sign that the day would go poorly was the argument at the breakfast table. Arthur Tewkesbury, livid after having been labeled "Crackers" by Cecil M. V. Halstead-Brown, regarding the Henley winner of 1831, flung down his napkin and ran headlong into the dining room's trompe-l'oeil mural, which depicted an open door leading to a meadow, with trees and a river.

William Worcester went down to the river, and took a single scull from the boathouse without inquiring into the condition of the shell.

NOW THE POINT OF THE GAME, DON'T YOU SEE, IS TO HAVE A 'BIT OF FUN'--WHAT?-- WITH A 'RACQUET' AND A BALL! VERY WELL...

At Noon, Major Wingfield Arrived and Taught Them the New Lawn Game

FAIR PLAY

WINGFIELD SEARS DWIGHT BROOKES LARNED McLOUGHLIN LACOSTE TILDEN BROWNE WILLS

By late afternoon, a new day had dawned in the history of lawn games. Within a year it had crossed the Atlantic, within a decade swept the globe.

Ahead lay Wimbledon, Forest Hills, Wright, Ditson, and the Davis Cup! However, Sir John remained firm in his belief that croquet was superior to tennis.

Album from the Attic: Tour of Europe, 1926

Aboard the Empress of Scotland

Venice

A flat tire at Lake Lucerne

Berlin

Alice and Don climbing Mont Blanc

Hotel Beaurivage (our room was on the other side)

Chamonix
(not the top)

Nancy met
a little
Dutch girl
in Amsterdam

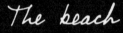

The beach

A friend
of Ed's from
Amherst and
his wife and
her sister
and aunt

Notre Dame
Cathedral,
or Amiens

Passing
the Caronia

On Labor Day, We Honor the Workingman and His Work

PITHECANTHROPUS SUDORIFICUS
The First Man to "Work,"
and a Real Hustler, Too

The Javanese
Go-Getter

Skull fragments found in 1937–38 indicate that Pith. Sud. had a brow 6 cm higher than Pith. Erec., suggesting a wide-awake attitude and a heavily furred coccygeal notochord (literally "bright-eyed and bushy-tailed"). It is believed that his "work" was primitive in nature—primarily throwing rocks for other people in exchange for breadfruit.

EARLY WORK—NORWAY
Probable example of prehistoric work. Stones appear to be piled in sequence of size and weight—largest at bottom, smallest at top.

The
Stones
of
Thrud

THE COFFEE BREAK
Statuary in Yucatan suggests that Mayan laborers were among first to initiate the "coffee break."

Figure of man resting with cup—Temple of Kukulcan, Chichén Itzá, Mexico

"GIVING UP"
Before work was fully understood and carried out, there were many attempts—doomed to failure. An example is the famous "Unfinished Horseshoe of the Nile."

The Unfinished Horseshoe of the Nile

VACATION
Once the idea of work was firmly entrenched, man labored three hundred sixty-five days of the year. It was Ed Burbank, a veteran wattle-wood worker, who conceived the idea of "taking some time off." He returned to the wattle-extract mill after two weeks at his uncle's farm in Ohio.

"Where the hell have *you* been?" demanded the boss.

"I've been on vacation," replied Ed.

"On *what?*"

"Vacation," said Ed, extracting wattle immediately.

"Oh," said the boss. Soon all the workers were taking two weeks off and going to Ed's uncle's farm in Ohio.

ALF, THE NEWCASTLE COAL HEAVER
Delivered six wagons of coal to Newcastle, 1851. "Don't blime me," he said. "I owney do as I'm told, see— nuffin' more."

Alf

GETTING "PAID"
Etruscan coin (with toothmarks, probably to verify authenticity). Coin discovered in vicinity of early ditch.

DELEGATING WORK
The Egyptian Pharaohs were among the first to understand that the man who conceptualizes the "work" need not be the one to execute it.

Honest Toil—Portion of mural in Oswegatchie, Conn., post office

"All værk and no play makes Nils a rötegröte med flüde."*

---Danish proverb

* Raspberry pudding

ROME—THE FIRST DAY (SUNSET)

Italian construction workers wisely resisted the "speed-up" and refused to complete the city on a rush basis. Their defiance gave courage to future generations of workers, and bequeathed a motto for all times: "Rome wasn't built in a day."

TECHNOLOGY

While playing one day with a six-dollar Meccano set, a distinguished engineer was struck with an idea that would alter the course of history. "If we could make one of these babies really *big,* it could help build things." Soon, huge Meccano cranes and stuff were etched across the sky of America.

LABOR STRIFE

The Battle of Nick's Barbershop, 1919: All Nick's barbers joined the union except old Howard (third chair down), who attempted sabotage by pouring witch hazel on customers' neckties and giving "butches" to everyone who asked for a "light trim."

OLDEST UNION MEMBER

Philip Rolph has been a member of the Truckers since 1907. Although ninety-six years old, he is still at the wheel. (His truck, unfortunately, has been stuck in a traffic jam on West 46th Street since last August, and Phil's license has expired.)

Philip Rolph at the wheel of his Mack rig

RECALCITRANT MANAGEMENT

Monroe Neon, president of Gibraltar Concrete, swore no union men would ever set foot in his plant. They never did. Union men led a destructive parade through his rhododendrons, however.

Neon

ELECTRICITY—GOOD OR BAD?

The advent of electricity has been both a blessing and a curse to the workingman. Many workers have detected slippage in the motivational area, declaring, "Why should *I* do it if electricity can do it?" Indifference and apathy increased after the invention of the dry-cell battery.

MACHINE VS. MAN
THE THREAT OF AUTOMATION

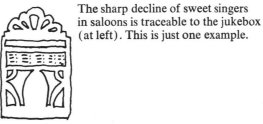

The sharp decline of sweet singers in saloons is traceable to the jukebox (at left). This is just one example.

OBSOLESCENCE

No sooner had man learned to "work" than he found, to his sorrow, that his "work" was sometimes not wanted. Brutmann, whose rosewood nutcrackers with inlaid elephant-tusk scenes from the Bible were the rage of Ghent, was "laid off" when frescoes caught on big.

Brutmann, the Wood-carver of Ghent

DECLINE OF INTEREST IN WORK

Familiar American saying—twentieth century. Suggests that work may be losing some of its appeal.

TAKE IT EASY !!

Pastry In Motion

A Rich History, Revealed Through Art and Archeology

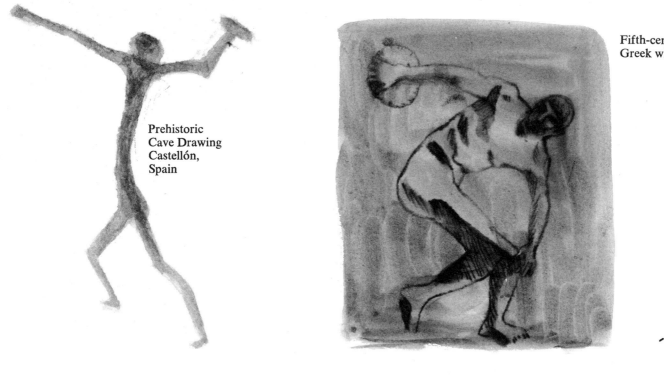

Prehistoric
Cave Drawing
Castellón,
Spain

Fifth-century
Greek with Pie

Crust Fragments,
Sumatra.
Carbon dated
1,000,000 B.C.

Egypt.
Eighteenth
dynasty—
pie-making,
delivery,
and throw

The Scientific Approach. Muybridge's Study of the Motion—1885

approach to pie   picking up pie   the throw

unidentified
picture
(not part of
same series)

Early designs by
Andrea del Verrocchio (1435–88)
for Colleoni statue
clearly establish use
of pasta in combat
during Renaissance

An Old-World Tradition
From England—
the *straight-arm
running bubble-
and-squeak pitch*
From Italy—
the *pizza toss*
and the diminutive
ravioli throw;
from Germany—
the *hard-hitting strudel;*
from Russia—
the *flying blintz;*
from France—
the delicate *crêpe fling*
and the *éclair heave;*
from Denmark—
the *wienerbrod barrage*
and the fast-moving
aebleskiver (doughnut)

1909: French officials and distinguished guests
attended a meet of the Patisserie Aeronautique

The Debacle on the Rue des Champs.
The Dessert
Table at
Les Trois Lapins

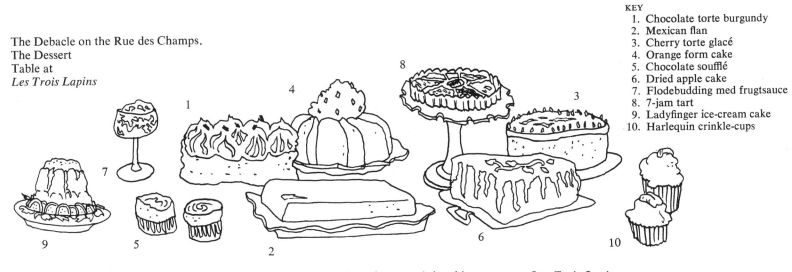

KEY
1. Chocolate torte burgundy
2. Mexican flan
3. Cherry torte glacé
4. Orange form cake
5. Chocolate soufflé
6. Dried apple cake
7. Flodebudding med frugtsauce
8. 7-jam tart
9. Ladyfinger ice-cream cake
10. Harlequin crinkle-cups

From *Le Monde,* October 24, 1921 (translation): "Gendarmes bravely entered the chic restaurant *Les Trois Lapins*
at 47 Rue des Champs yesterday in a gallant attempt to restore order in the midst of a full-scale pastry riot [*débâcle
de patisserie*]. Captain Henri de Flange, of the 16th Arrondissement Préfecture, was struck full in the face by a ladyfinger ice-cream cake[9], and his men met a hail of harlequin crinkle-cups[10] as they advanced. The proprietor, M.
Chambray, had been rendered helpless by a swiftly delivered Mexican flan[2]. . . ."

Post-Napoleonic Period.
Steam-driven mortar capable of firing 1500 isceler torteletten
(almond butter cookies) per hour, 1816

**In America,
the Pie Reaches
Its Apex**
For the
frontiersman,
dedication to
the sport meant
many lonely
hours of
watchful waiting

Unidentified Flying Pies in Sports Events

How the
Australians
Lost in 1926.
(Aussie's error
in aerodynamics
caused surprising
"boomerang" effect)

Smith College fielded a
team in 1919.

The *Resolute* defeated
Shamrock IV 3–2 in the
1920 America's Cup
Races. Note flying pie
near top jib (believed
thrown by Sir Thomas
Lipton during close reach
—a clean miss,
apparently, owing to
windward trajectory).

In America, There Is a Sense of Time, Place, and the Fitness of Things
A recipient in a state of maximum readiness (note folded umbrella, pocket handkerchief, boutonniere, Sulka shirt with collar pin, tie clip with New York Yacht Club insigne, etc.), properly positioned—i.e., hailing a taxi in front of the Downtown Association. Recipient has made self eligible for . . . a custard pie.

The Pie Has Kept Pace with a Growing Technology

Safety has become a major concern. Ralph Nader study of impact of pie on target (clean miss)

The American Pie in the Space Age

It's an American dream: to put an honest-to-goodness old-fashioned home-baked apple pie on the moon.

Can we do it?
The experts say . . .
yes!

Astronaut Merlet "Skeech" Heff

Apple pie resting
on the Sea of
Tranquility
(artist's conception)

The First Decade 1929–1939

WHEN THE SIMPSONS CAME TO DINNER, MR. SIMPSON DID MAGIC TRICKS FOR US BEFORE WE HAD TO GO TO BED.

THE TREES WERE ENORMOUS, AND, BEING MAPLES, UNCLIMABLE. THE LEAVES WERE DENSE AND GREEN, AND THERE WERE ALWAYS SHADOWS ON THE SIDEWALK.

TWO BLOCKS AWAY THERE WAS A MEADOW WITH A COW IN IT.

MY PARENTS WENT OUT WEST FOR A TRIP. THEY TOOK MY BROTHER, BUT I WAS TOO YOUNG. I CRIED, BUT WHEN THEY CAME BACK, THEY BROUGHT ME A REAL COWBOY HAT FROM CHEYENNE, WYOMING.

IN THE LATE AFTERNOON, THERE WAS THE RADIO.

THE RADIO WAS GOTHIC IN DESIGN, WITH A TAPESTRY-LIKE CLOTH IN THE APERTURES, QUITE LOOSE. WHEN TURNED ON, THE DIAL WOULD LIGHT UP, THE RADIO SLOWLY WARMED UP, AND THEN WE WOULD LISTEN TO WJZ – THE BLUE NETWORK – OR OTHER STATIONS, FOR "THE SHADOW," "LITTLE ORPHAN ANNIE," "BUCK ROGERS IN THE 21ST CENTURY."

FIRST FOOTBALL

LOVED SHEILA WEINBERG AT SCHOOL. (IF SHE HAD TO EAT BEETS, SHE CRIED.)

BUT NOT RUTHIE NEXT DOOR. SHE WAS PRISSY.

AND THE JANGLE OF IT.

FIRST DOG. REMEMBER TEXTURE OF HAIR, GLEAM OF DOG LICENSE ON RED COLLAR, HE GOT HIT BY CAR WHEN OLD. REMEMBER BLOOD ON BLACK COAT.

FROM A FRIEND OF THE FAMILY. DON'T REMEMBER THE MAN, BUT WHEN HEARING THE NAME ALWAYS SAY TO SELF "HE GAVE ME THE FOOTBALL."

THE BELL DIDN'T WORK

THE FUNNIEST THING WAS WHEN LOU THOMAS PUT A GINGERSNAP IN HIS EYE LIKE A MONOCLE AND SAID – IN A BRITISH ACCENT – "THEY DO IT MUCH BETTER IN LONDON." WE DIED, AND MADE HIM DO IT AGAIN AND AGAIN.

GRANDPA (THE TALL ONE WITH THE HIGH COLLAR) DIED. WE HAD TO BE QUIET AROUND THE HOUSE.

ON THE FOURTH OF JULY, THERE WAS ONE KIND OF FIRECRACKER THAT SPUTTERED AND RACED ALONG THE GROUND, AND WE WERE TOLD IT WOULD CHASE YOU.

BUT THE BIKE COULD DO THINGS NOBODY ELSE'S COULD.

TOY CARS WERE MADE OF CAST-IRON

RALPH WORKED FOR A FAMILY DOWN THE BLOCK. HE WASHED THEIR CAR WITH A BIG SPONGE, AND THE GARAGE FLOOR WOULD BE AWASH WITH SOAPSUDS. EVERY TIME JOE LOUIS FOUGHT, RALPH WOULD BET ON LOUIS, AND I WOULD HAVE TO TAKE BILLY CONN OR WHOEVER, AND LOSE 10¢.

THERE WERE TWO WAYS TO GO ANYWHERE: THE ORDINARY WAY, AND THE SHORT-CUT.

(DUGAN) THE BAKERY TRUCK WOULD DRIVE UP, AND THE MAN WOULD KNOCK ON THE DOOR, AND YELL:

DUGANS!!

HEARD YEHUDI MENUHIN AT CARNEGIE HALL. VERY LATE AT NIGHT. AFTER THAT, I TOOK VIOLIN LESSONS FOR A WHILE FROM MISS HEFLIN.

MY OLDER BROTHER SEEMED TO KNOW A LOT OF BIG SECRETS, AND HIS DAYS WERE FULL OF MYSTERIOUS, IMPORTANT & CONFIDENTIAL MISSIONS.

DIARY

ON HIS CLOSET SHELF, HE KEPT A DIARY, AND LOCKED IT WITH A KEY. WHEN I FINALLY FOUND THE KEY AND OPENED IT UP, I DISCOVERED ALL THE ENTRIES WERE NEARLY IDENTICAL: "GOT UP, HAD BREAKFAST. WENT TO SCHOOL. CAME HOME. HAD SUPPER. WENT TO BED."

THE CAR WAS BLUE AND IT HAD A RUMBLE SEAT, AND WE ALWAYS ASKED, "CAN WE SIT IN THE RUMBLE?" WE USUALLY COULD.

ONE HOUSE TO STAY AWAY FROM WAS MRS. DODDS'. SHE HAD ORANGE HAIR, AND WAS OLD, AND SHE USED TO CALL THE FIRE DEPARTMENT TO COMPLAIN THAT MEN WERE RIDING BICYCLES ON HER ROOF.

AND ON VALENTINE'S DAY SNEAKED UP TO HELEN THOMPSON'S HOUSE (SHE WAS 14) AND LEFT A HAND-MADE ANONYMOUS CARD THAT SAID "GOSH, I THINK YOU'RE BEAUTIFUL!" AND RAN.

FELL OFF A HIGH STONE WALL, HAD TO GO TO THE HOSPITAL FOR WHAT SEEMED LIKE A MONTH.

ACE

WE READ "BIG-LITTLE BOOKS" AND COMICS. THE JOHNSON-SMITH CATALOGUE OFFERED AN ASTONISHING VARIETY OF WONDERS. YOU COULD SEND AWAY FOR A VENTRILOQUIST KIT, OR THE ART OF SELF-DEFENSE; ALMOST ANYTHING. THE SUSPENSE OF WAITING CARRIED US THROUGH SEVERAL WEEKS, WITH NOTHING ELSE ON OUR MIND.

THERE WAS A MOVIE IN THE NEXT TOWN. UNLESS THERE WAS A SHIRLEY TEMPLE, IT WAS

VERY RARE TO GO TO THE MOVIES.* BUT GRANDPA TOOK ME TO "THREE LITTLE PIGS." AT RADIO CITY MUSIC HALL. HE WAS QUITE OLD. HE TOOK THE ESCALATOR IN THE LOBBY.

* WE SAW A SERIAL THERE, WHICH HAD A SHADOW OF A HUGE SPIDER ON THE WALL, AND A FEARFUL VILLAIN WHO WAS UNSEEN BUT COULD BE HEARD DRAGGING ONE FOOT. FOR THE NEXT FEW YEARS, I NEVER WENT TO SLEEP WITHOUT FIRST DECLARING TO MYSELF I WOULD NOT THINK ABOUT THAT MOVIE.

MY FATHER WOULD PLAY THE BUGLE, BUT NOT OFTEN ENOUGH. HE WOULD HOLD A TOWEL OVER THE END SO IT WOULDN'T BE TOO LOUD.

MADE FUN OF PETE K. AT SCHOOL, AND MADE HIM CRY. FIRST TIME I KNEW YOU COULD HURT SOMEONE'S FEELINGS. HAD FOUGHT WITH KIDS A LOT BEFORE, BUT WITH PETE I HADN'T EVEN TOUCHED HIM.

WE BUILT A DAM OF MUD AND STICKS AND STONES IN A BROOK NEAR SCHOOL. THE BEST TIME I EVER HAD.

SAW THE NORTHERN LIGHTS ONE NIGHT

WE WENT TO BAKER FIELD AND SAW SID LUCKMAN THROW TOUCHDOWN PASSES FOR COLUMBIA, AND WE GOT A LIGHT BLUE PENNANT TO BRING HOME. IT WAS SOMETHING YOU COULD LOOK AT FOR A LONG TIME.

IT WAS HARD TO GO TO SLEEP IN THE SUMMER, BECAUSE, OUT THE WINDOW, THERE WAS THE SOUND OF THINGS STILL GOING ON.

VITO WAS A GARDENER. HIS LUNCH WAS USUALLY A LOAF OF ITALIAN BREAD WITH SALAMI IN IT, WRAPPED IN THE DAILY NEWS. I'LL NEVER FORGET THE SMELL. HE TOLD ME STORIES ABOUT HIS FRIENDS AND THE WORLD, ABOUT VOLUNTEER FIREMEN, WHORE HOUSES, EVERYTHING. HE COULD MAKE PLANTS GROW, AND HE WOULD SPLICE BRANCHES TO MAKE HYBRIDS. I REMEMBER HIM CROUCHING BY A COLD FRAME, PEERING AT THE SMALL SHOOTS AND FINGERING THE DIRT. "FLOWERS, FLOWERS," HE SANG TO HIMSELF, "SOON, SOON."

LUNCH

WE THREW A HANDFUL OF PEBBLES AT A CAR ONE DAY, AND TO OUR HORROR, THE DRIVER SLAMMED ON HIS BRAKES. WE RAN HOME & UPSTAIRS, AND HID UNDER A BED, AND THEN WE HEARD THE LOW RUMBLE OF THE MAN'S VOICE, TALKING TO OUR MOTHER AT THE FRONT DOOR.

AS A CHRISTMAS CARD,

$1.00

THE MAN DOWN THE BLOCK GAVE US A RUBBER DOLLAR BILL, BECAUSE HE DIDN'T LIKE ROOSEVELT. MY FAMILY DIDN'T THINK THAT WAS FUNNY.

WHEN YOU PEELED THE PAPER OFF THE TOP OF THE DIXIE CUP, THERE WOULD BE A PICTURE OF HOOT GIBSON OR RAMON NAVARRO.

WE STOOD SHIVERING ON THE LAWN IN COATS AND PAJAMAS THE NIGHT THE HARMON'S HOUSE CAUGHT FIRE.

THE BEST THING OF ALL WAS PROBABLY ONE DAY IN SUMMER WHEN THE ZEPPELIN HINDENBURG SLOWLY PASSED DIRECTLY OVER OUR HOUSE.

200th Anniversary Photograph

Near Misses

Outstanding Examples of Americans Who, on the Very Doorstep of Success, Found Failure

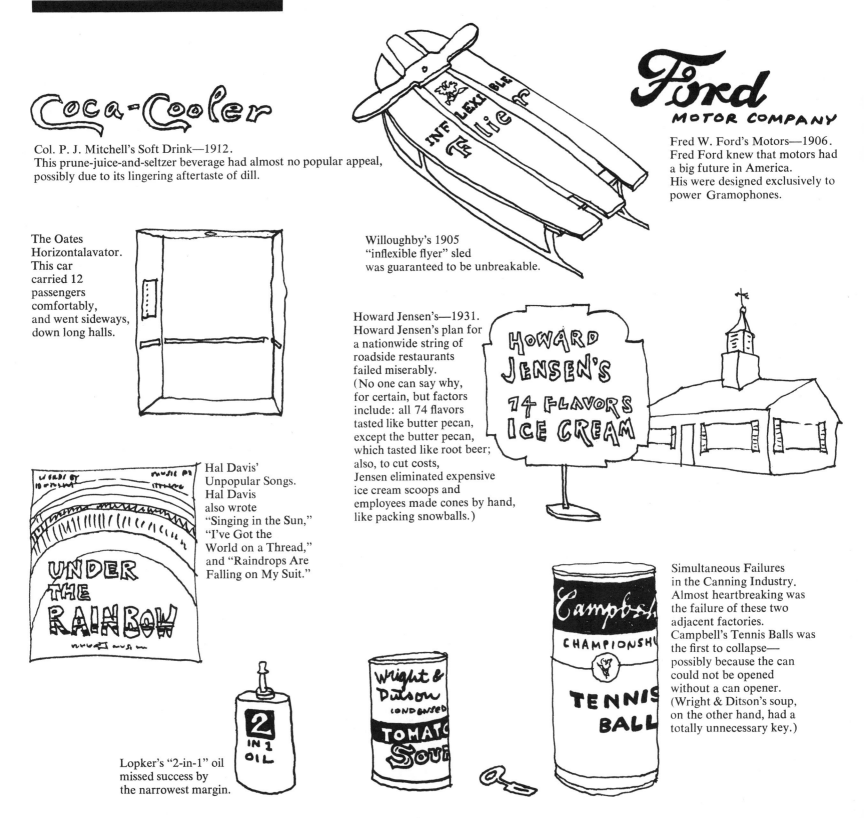

Coca-Cooler

Col. P. J. Mitchell's Soft Drink—1912.
This prune-juice-and-seltzer beverage had almost no popular appeal, possibly due to its lingering aftertaste of dill.

Ford MOTOR COMPANY

Fred W. Ford's Motors—1906.
Fred Ford knew that motors had a big future in America.
His were designed exclusively to power Gramophones.

The Oates Horizontalavator. This car carried 12 passengers comfortably, and went sideways, down long halls.

Willoughby's 1905 "inflexible flyer" sled was guaranteed to be unbreakable.

Howard Jensen's—1931.
Howard Jensen's plan for a nationwide string of roadside restaurants failed miserably.
(No one can say why, for certain, but factors include: all 74 flavors tasted like butter pecan, except the butter pecan, which tasted like root beer; also, to cut costs, Jensen eliminated expensive ice cream scoops and employees made cones by hand, like packing snowballs.)

HOWARD JENSEN'S 74 FLAVORS ICE CREAM

Hal Davis' Unpopular Songs. Hal Davis also wrote "Singing in the Sun," "I've Got the World on a Thread," and "Raindrops Are Falling on My Suit."

WORDS BY / MUSIC BY

UNDER THE RAINBOW

Simultaneous Failures in the Canning Industry. Almost heartbreaking was the failure of these two adjacent factories. Campbell's Tennis Balls was the first to collapse—possibly because the can could not be opened without a can opener. (Wright & Ditson's soup, on the other hand, had a totally unnecessary key.)

Campbell CHAMPIONSHIP TENNIS BALL

Wright & Ditson CONDENSED TOMATO SOUP

2 IN 1 OIL

Lopker's "2-in-1" oil missed success by the narrowest margin.

August Morn by Kluckhorn—1878.
Kluckhorn's lovely paintings invariably misjudged the public's taste by a
mere fraction (*August Morn*—too much scenery, not enough girl).

Lucy Murtagh's
1963 study of
Irish geology
sold only 4 copies.

The Indian Problem: Annals of Law and Order

Before
1650 (partial)

Sunday Morning Inspection, Fort Huachuca, Arizona

9th Cavalry, Fort Robinson, Nebraska

Colonel J. M. Chivington
(former minister)
(Sand Creek, Colorado,
massacre, 1864—slaughtered 500 Cheyennes,
mostly women and children,
who had been guaranteed
military protection)

Soldiers Bringing Up 12-pound Napoleon Guns for Winter Campaign Against Sitting Bull and Crazy Horse, 1867

Red Cloud
Sioux Chief

Report of Major Downing—Punitive Expedition Against the Cheyenne

We started about eleven o'clock in the day, traveled all day and all that night — about daylight I succeeded in surprising the Cheyenne village of Cedar Bluffs... We commenced shooting. I ordered the men to commence killing them. They lost, as I am informed, some twenty-six killed and sixty wounded. My own loss was one killed and one wounded. I burnt up their lodges and everything I could get hold of. I took no prisoners. We got out of ammunition and could not pursue them.

U.S. Commissioners and Indian Chiefs in Council at Fort Laramie, 1868

Colonel George A. Custer

Colonel Custer, His Officers, and Their Families in Camp

Bones of Horses, Graves of Unknown Soldiers at Little Big Horn

Sitting Bull and His Family Under Guard at Fort Randall, 1882

Sitting Bull Just Before His Death

General George Crook

Apaches

Looking Glass
(Nez Percés)
(killed during
Joseph's retreat,
1877)

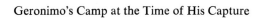

Geronimo's Camp at the Time of His Capture

Surrendered Apaches at Fort Bowie

Chief Joseph

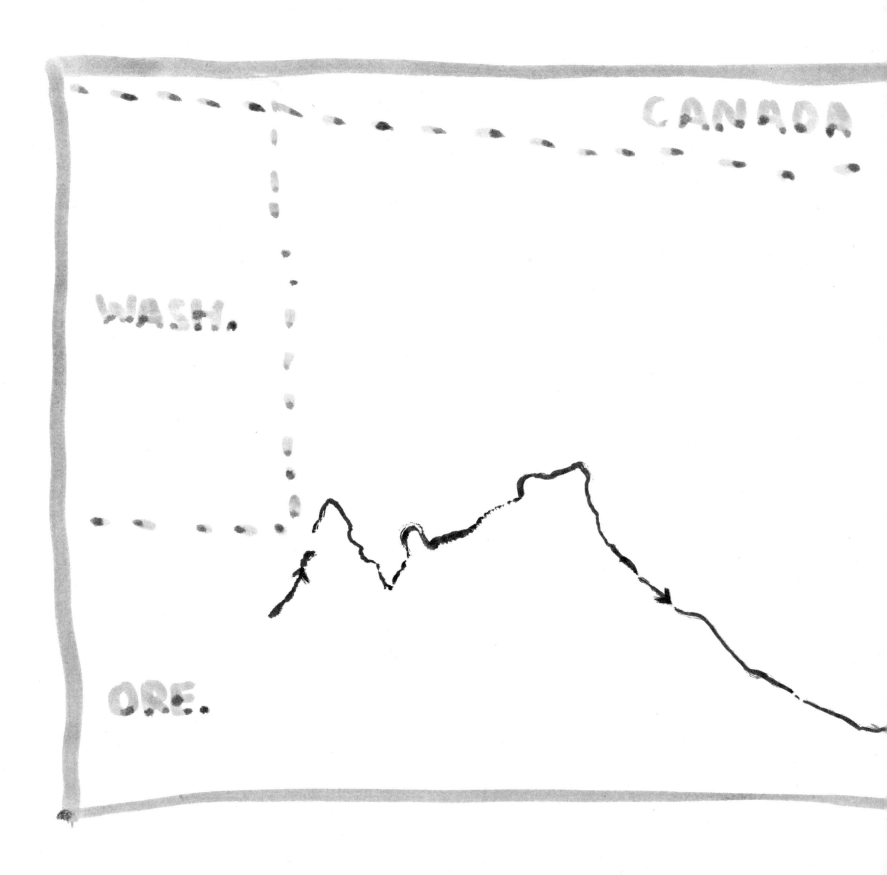

CANADA

WASH.

ORE.

SURRENDER OCTOBER 5 1877

WYO.

General Oliver Otis Howard
(pursued Chief Joseph)

Retreat of
the Nez Percés
under Chief Joseph

General Nelson A. Miles

Chief Joseph's
Speech of Surrender
to General Miles

I AM TIRED OF FIGHTING OUR CHIEFS ARE KILLED
LOOKING GLASS IS DEAD TOOHOOLHOOLZOTE IS
DEAD THE OLD MEN ARE ALL DEAD IT IS THE
YOUNG MEN WHO SAY YES OR NO HE WHO LED
THE YOUNG MEN IS DEAD IT IS COLD AND WE
HAVE NO BLANKETS THE LITTLE CHILDREN
ARE FREEZING TO DEATH MY PEOPLE SOME
OF THEM HAVE RUN AWAY TO THE HILLS AND
HAVE NO BLANKETS NO FOOD NO ONE KNOWS
WHERE THEY ARE PERHAPS FREEZING TO
DEATH I WANT TO HAVE TIME TO LOOK FOR
MY CHILDREN AND SEE HOW MANY I CAN
FIND MAYBE I SHALL FIND THEM AMONG
THE DEAD HEAR ME MY CHIEFS I AM
TIRED MY HEART IS SICK AND SAD
FROM WHERE THE SUN STANDS NOW I WILL
FIGHT NO MORE FOREVER

Wounded Knee Creek, South Dakota, December 1890
(Over 200 Sioux men, women, and children
killed by 7th Cavalry using Hotchkiss guns.
Many wounded, left on the field,
froze to death in blizzard the next night.)
The end of Indian resistance in America.

The Tree in the Park

THE PARK:

The park consists of sixteen acres of land projecting south into Long Island Sound and bounded on the north by the tracks of the Penn Central railroad. A third of the land forms a promontory, ending in a steep cliff that falls directly to the water, fifty feet below, or to a narrow, rocky beach, depending on the tide. To the west is a broad sand beach and a large parking lot. To the east there is a meadow rising from the shore; at the summit, the tall grass has been cut to lawn, and here there are slides and swings and seesaws, picnic tables, places to build fires, and, near the edge of the cliff, several enormous beech trees.

THE GATE:

The gate to the park is locked early in the morning; the park does not open until nine, and the entire area is surrounded by a high chain-link fence—except on the water sides. When the gate is opened at nine, there is a guard on duty in a small sentry box next to the gate, and he checks the incoming cars to see if they have a pass proving that they live in this town. If they do, they may park their cars in the parking lot; all others are turned away. The guard is usually an old man. If his authority were defied, he would not, most likely, resort to force; there is a telephone in the sentry box, and he would call for help. But, for those who desire it, there are other ways and times to get into the park.

HOW TO GET INTO THE PARK EARLY IN THE MORNING WITHOUT SWIMMING, BOATING, OR CLIMBING THE FENCE:

Drive to the parking lot behind the supermarket, near the railroad tracks, where the abandoned freight station stands. Park at the edge of the lot, where the field of wild flowers used to begin (mostly chicory); now it's a car wash. Take off your shoes and socks and leave them in the car. Walk to the tracks. Look left and right; you can see for a mile or more in both directions here. To the east, the tracks curve around the bay, and there is an old black drawbridge where they cross the river. When the bridge is open (to let the boats in and out of the river), it tips up in the air, leaving a great space. If a train were to come roaring down from Boston—even a high-speed train—it is unlikely that it could go up the sharply inclined track, leap the abyss, and land accurately enough on this side to continue in this direction. There is little danger, then, from the east—while the bridge is open. The bridge is now open. To the west, there is a clear view of more than a mile, perhaps two miles, as the tracks pass through a series of cuts on the way to New York. There is danger from this direction, but frequent glances—and perhaps an awareness of the vibrations through the soles of the feet—should suffice. While you are looking out for trains, you will notice that everything on or near the tracks tends toward the same color and value—a yellowish-brown rust. The old freight building is this hue; so are the stones between the ties. The entire area appears to have been washed with sepia; this makes the wild flowers brilliant, the water in the sound dazzling.

Walking along railroad tracks with bare feet is not the most comfortable form of travel in the world. On the other hand, comfort is the enemy of discovery. The tracks, moreover, are the best route here; on the inland side, there is tall grass and garbage and broken glass; on the water side, huge boulders are frozen in their tumble down to the sound. Walking between the ties—on the stone chips, or gravel—is the least satisfactory. The stones have sharp edges and points; there is little to be said for the stones. Even a limited amount of walking on them will cause the barefoot walker to switch to (a) the ties or (b) the rails.

The ties (a) are not bad. They are stained and oily, but they are wood, with handsome splits and splinters and cracks. The major problem is the spacing of the ties. They are too close together for a normal stride, and if you skip a tie—i.e., step from Tie No. 1 to Tie No. 3—it is a little too far. If you insist on tie-walking, you have a choice of two strange-looking and uncomfortable paces. You can alternate them, or whatever, but presently you will be tempted to try (b) the rails. Walking along a rail is not boring. It requires agility. Again, two modes are possible: going very *slowly,* placing one foot sideways, then the other foot the other way, or going very *fast,* with both feet placed alternately in a forward direction, until you lose your balance and fall.

Since both forms of rail-walking, like both styles of tie-walking are peculiar, uncomfortable, and undignified, the best solution is probably a combination walk, utilizing a sequential pattern of all forms—ties, gravel, rails—none of which is satisfactory in itself but each of which is, at least temporarily, a relief from the previous style.

Shortly (provided you have not failed to look up and down the tracks during the preceding), you will arrive at a point where you should shift to the shoulder. Here the tracks cross an underpass, but to your left there are large blocks of stone on which you can climb down to the shore. Descend cautiously. There is a low telephone line and a rusted broken wire fence. Walk beside the fence slowly; it has jagged edges. On the shore, you may have to wade to get around the edge of the fence, depending on the tide. The rocks are slippery, so it is well to have left your shoes behind; if you fall, you will need both hands free. Once around the fence, you climb a sandy path that parallels the tracks for a while, then turns and goes out along the shoulder of the promontory. The water is below you, to your left, and straight ahead. You are now in the park. Turn to your right and walk through a long meadow of tall grass; it sweeps gently toward the top of the bluff and the beech trees. Take your time.

THE BEECH TREE ON THE BLUFF:

It would be very hard to count precisely the number of initials carved on this vast tree. Over the years, some lacerations have healed; others have merged and blurred or grown monstrous, twenty feet above the ground. Is that an "R" or a "B"—or a "P" with a period? The spectator, viewing the hieroglyphic hearts, is apt to wonder about love. Those four initials inside that heart on the bottom of that branch: Did they love each other? Do they now? Was it carved in the moment of discovery, or in hope, or to prop up a failing union? Were there two people there—one in the branches, one on the ground? Or did one cut the letters without consent? Did he deny it later, or show it proudly? Did he lead her by the hand through that meadow and then, standing in the beech tree's shadow on a hot day, point overhead to what he had done? Which ones have parted, which ones stayed together? Which ones bear scars, together or apart? Do any of them ever come to this tree and look, to see if their mark has healed or grown?

One afternoon last week, late afternoon, two middle-aged ladies sat on two straight-hanging metal swings, gossiping, their hair in large pink curlers, while, on either side, children flung themselves into the sky and back, their swings screeching with each passage, and the ladies said, "She said . . ." "She *did?*" Not far away, sitting at one of the picnic tables, a man cradled his head on his folded arms, resting on the sticky varnished surface. Paper plates, with smears of ketchup on the white, lay in the grass. Were these people's initials on this tree—or on some other tree? The ladies, gathering up the children, may have glanced through the leaves in passing and kept it to themselves, what they saw there. The man sleeps; what initials form within his dreams?

A light breeze came, and the leaves on the beech tree moved idly, their heart shapes—light green on one side, darker on the other—cut across the blues of the sound and sky. They have perhaps three months before they fall.

The Beech Tree

71 72 73 74 75 10 9 8 7 6 5 4 3 2 1